MAKE ME BEG

JULIE KRISS

Join Julie's new release newsletter

PROLOGUE

Ten Years Ago
Lauren

THERE WAS nothing worse than being a girl who had never been kissed. At twelve, it was expected. At fourteen, it was sort of weird. And at sixteen, it was a state of emergency.

Nothing. No experiments behind the school at way too young an age. No spin-the-bottle dares. No sweet, gentle boy putting his lips on mine for the first time, even for a second. Nada.

The lack of it kept me up at night. My fraternal twin sister, Emily, had definitely been kissed—the first was Chad Kemper, who had dated her for two weeks when we were fifteen. She'd had other boyfriends since then, been kissed other times. She told me everything. In return I made up a story that Michael Porter and I made out at last year's Spring Fling dance, but it had to stay top secret because he was dating Heather Klem. Emily thought that was thrilling.

I hadn't made out with Michael Porter. Or anyone. I couldn't say what the problem was. I was just as pretty as Emily, though in a different way—Emily was blonde and outgoing, and I was the quieter one, my hair a darker honey color. I wasn't hideous, and I thought I had a half-decent personality. I was smart, I got along with people, and I made sure I always looked and smelled good.

But Emily was popular. I liked to call her a drama queen, but she was a risk-taker. She was confident, she was never shy, and she liked to get out there and have fun.

I tried to be more like Emily, but I hated risk. It made my stomach turn. Boys—teenage boys—were risky. What if I met one that was mean? A bad kisser? What if he told his friends about me? What if he laughed behind my back? What if he wanted sex after the first kiss? What would I do then?

I couldn't get near enough to any of them to try anything. I just couldn't. And now I was paying the price, because oh, God, I was sixteen and I wanted to be kissed so badly.

So tonight I'd taken a risk.

I was standing in the Riggs house—the most infamous house in Westlake, Michigan, home of the Riggs brothers, on the wrong side of the tracks. I had never been in the Riggs house in my life, and my mother, who was a cop, would have a heart attack if she knew. Which was why I'd told her I was going to my friend Taylor's house tonight—and, because I was a good girl who had never given her any trouble, she believed me.

But I wasn't just in the Riggs house. I was at one of Dex Riggs' parties.

Dex Riggs was the oldest Riggs brother, and the worst. At seventeen he was the despair of every teacher at Westlake High. He was the guy at school who could get you anything—weed, pills, faked absence slips, swiped test answers. He rarely went to class. He got into bars even though he was underage without ever getting caught. Fights seemed to follow him wherever he went—and he always won. Guys hated him—because they secretly wished they were him—and girls were a little scared of him. Not because Dex was threatening, but because he was too much.

The other Riggs brothers, especially Ryan, were exciting bad boy fun. But Dex Riggs was the equivalent of putting a shot into your pint of beer. You didn't need it; you'd probably survive it; but you might wish you hadn't.

And of course, Dex Riggs' parties were legendary.

This one was loud. Crazy loud. Music pulsed from the stereo downstairs in the living room, nearly shaking the place. I didn't know the song; I was a top-40 girl. There was a beer pong competition that was getting roars of appreciation. People had spilled out into the back yard, where someone was throwing up, and more people had spilled out the front, where they were racing bicycles up and down the street—in the snow.

I had had two wine coolers. I had talked to the people I knew, which was a lot of them—Westlake wasn't a very big place. I had done some dancing, maybe a little flirting. Now my head throbbed and I had to pee, and I still hadn't been kissed.

The downstairs bathroom was occupied—with more than one person, I thought—so I made my way upstairs, feeling along the dim corridor. The music still boomed up here, a resounding vibration, though the voices were quieter. The Riggs house was big—it had been a rich man's house a long time ago, though now it was run-down—and there were a lot of rooms. It took me a few tries to find the bathroom.

I came out, running my hands through my long hair. I was wearing snug jeans, an old T-shirt, and ankle boots, with very little makeup. I knew better than to overdress for a Riggs party.

Still, coming here wasn't getting me any more kissed than I'd been a few hours ago. I thought about going home.

A door opened down the corridor and Dex Riggs came out.

He was a picture of bad boy perfection: worn jeans, black tee, dark tousled hair. He even had a shadow of stubble on his jaw, something a lot of his fellow seventeen-year-olds were desperately trying to achieve. He was alone. He closed the door quietly behind him, and then he saw me and gave me a smile that was understated and still somehow gorgeous. "Parker," he said.

I wondered what was in the room he'd just come out of. A girl? More than one? Something else? I burned with curiosity. I wanted to ask him, but instead I said, "Did you call me Parker because you don't know which sister I am?"

Dex rolled his eyes as if this was a stupid question. "Okay, *Lauren* Parker. Is that better?"

I shrugged, trying to look indifferent. But it was better. Dex Riggs knew my name.

"Lauren Parker," he said, "you crashed my party."

"I didn't know it was invite only," I shot back.

That made him laugh, a sound that sent shivers straight through my body, vibrating between my legs. He looked really, really good when he laughed. I had to force myself not to stare at the hard curve of his biceps where they emerged from his T-shirt sleeves. I wanted to put my hands on them. I wanted to feel if his skin was warm.

All of my risk-averse alarm bells went off, somewhere far away in my brain. And I didn't move.

He came closer. His eyes were dark blue, an amazing color I'd never seen on anyone else. There was a smear of something dark on the side of his neck, just above the collar of his shirt, and for a second I thought it was ink. *Why does Dex Riggs have an ink smear on him?* I wondered, and then I looked again and realized it was a bruise.

Dex caught me looking and raised a hand, tracing his fingertips over the bruise. He took another step closer.

"What's that from?" I asked him, taking a step back.

"Walked into a door," he said, coming closer still. I knew that the Riggs brothers lived alone with their father. None of them had a mother—she had taken off when the brothers were little. Their father ran an auto repair shop in town, and frankly he was a little terrifying. There didn't seem to be much parenting going on. Dex had come to school with bruises before, some of them old, some of them new. People said the bruises were from fights. But I wondered.

He dropped his hand from his neck. I stepped back again until my back was against the wall. Dex didn't seem to mind. He just came closer, putting his hands on the wall on either side of my head and caging me in.

"You having fun?" he asked me.

"I suppose," I managed, trying not to breathe him in. Failing.

He leaned closer. His body was nearly touching mine. I could have gotten away, but the thought didn't even cross my mind until he said his next words: "Good, because you're leaving."

I blinked, surprised. "Leaving?"

"We have about fifteen minutes before someone calls the cops," he said. "Someone always calls the cops. You want to be here when that happens?"

I felt my face go numb. My mother was a cop. No, I didn't want to get caught here when the cops came.

"I didn't think so," Dex said as if I'd spoken. "So I'm kicking you out, Parker. But now that I think about it, I'm going to do something first."

His eyes. How were they dark blue? How were his lashes so dark? How had I never noticed it in school? How was my heart pounding this hard just because one guy was this close to me? "What are you going to do?" I asked him.

He leaned in, his lips nearly brushing mine, and I felt the sizzle of it straight up my spine and down between my legs. "Come here and find out," he said, and he cupped my jaw with one hand and kissed me.

Holy shit. Holy, holy, *holy shit.*

It wasn't sweet or tentative or fumbling. It was nothing like a first kiss should be. Dex leaned me back against the wall, opened my mouth, and licked me like he was tasting me.

Every nerve ending in my body went off like a rocket. To my amazement I kissed him back, opening my mouth for him and floating on the sensation of it. I did it like I'd kissed a hundred boys before, or like I'd kissed Dex Riggs a hundred times. I curled my hands into the hem of his black T-shirt and held on.

He was warm. He tasted good—I couldn't even say what the flavor was, just that I liked it. I'd never had a man's tongue in my mouth before, but it was the hottest, most natural thing in the world to have Dex Riggs taste me. He kissed me like he knew every inch of me, like he knew what I liked and he wanted to do it. He didn't even put his hands on me, as if he knew that would be too much. He just let his mouth do everything.

We kissed like that for a long time, and when he broke the kiss I felt a terrible stab of disappointment. I was hot all over, burning in the best way. I wanted to do that some more. I wanted to do that for *hours.*

As I stood there speechless, trying to put the crumbs of my brain back together, Dex said, "We're done, Parker. Go get your coat and get out."

I was so weak and helpless I said, "Can we do that again?"

"Will I get arrested if we do?"

I couldn't lie. My mother would lose her shit if she knew what I'd just done. She'd probably throw Dex in jail for the rest of his natural life. "Yes."

"Then no." Dex dropped his hands from the wall. "Get the fuck out," he said, and walked away.

I stood there for a long minute before I finally obeyed him.

I had just been kissed for the first time at long last. And it was spectacular.

It also hurt.

It was only years later that I realized it was supposed to.

ONE

Present Day
Lauren

DAMN DEX RIGGS.

Damn, damn, damn him.

It was my sister's wedding day. Twenty after one in the afternoon. Emily was getting married at three; I was the maid of honor. And the groom's brother, the best man—Dex Riggs—was nowhere to be found.

"He'll show," Emily said. We were in the master bedroom of the old Riggs house, down the hall from that kiss ten years ago. A century ago. This was the room Dex had come out of, in fact. Emily was in a chair and Danielle, the stylist from the hair salon I owned, was twisting her blonde hair into a beautiful updo. "At least, I think he will."

I closed my eyes, trying to rein in my temper. Georgie, our makeup artist, took the opportunity to do an extra dusting of my lids. "I can't freaking believe he's not here," I said. "Have we tried calling him again?"

"Only twenty times." Emily was keeping it together, but her jaw was a little tight. She was marrying Luke Riggs, the love of her life, today and the only thing that had gone wrong was the absence of the best man. "Luke banged on the door of the guest house, and so did Jace. His car is there, but Dex doesn't answer."

"Jeez," Georgie said, dabbing powder to my chin. "Do you think there's something wrong? Maybe he's dead."

"He'd better be dead," I said.

Georgie looked surprised at how seriously I said it. But she didn't know Dex.

"We don't need to make a big deal of it," said Tara Montgomery, one of the other bridesmaids. She was sliding her feet into her high-heeled shoes. "The best man doesn't do much, really. The wedding will happen with or without him."

"He's stressing Emily out," I said.

"No, *you're* stressing me out," Emily corrected me. "I'm not marrying Dex, I'm marrying Luke. And Luke is here. I'm good."

I opened my mouth to argue, but Tara was giving me a firm look. Behind her, our other bridesmaid, Kate, was watching wide-eyed. Kate was new to Westlake and didn't know the history. She didn't know Dex.

Neither did I, really. Until the engagement announcement a few weeks ago, I hadn't seen Dex in years. He'd left for Detroit after high school, shocking everyone by becoming a cop. But he wasn't a cop anymore. Rumor said he'd crashed and burned. Now he was back in Westlake, living in the guest house behind the main house. Where he currently was, instead of being out here in the wedding party.

Except for that one wild kiss when I was sixteen, the first kiss I'd ever had, I knew nothing about Dex Riggs anymore. Except my gut told me he hadn't crashed and burned the way everyone thought he did. I couldn't say how I knew; I just knew. I wondered what had really happened. I wondered if Dex was okay.

Which didn't prevent me from wanting to kill him right now.

Since I'd last seen Dex, I'd started and run my own business for six years. I'd been married and divorced. I could handle a lot of things going wrong; I did it on a daily basis. But Dex Riggs' particular brand of chaos always did me in. I didn't feel in control when I thought about him. And that had to end. Especially today.

I stood up. "I'll fix this," I said.

Emily narrowed her eyes at me. She might be sappy on her wedding day, but she was my fraternal twin, we'd shared a uterus, and she knew me better than anyone. "How, exactly?"

"I'm going into the guest house to get him. Isn't there a spare key?"

"In the kitchen," Emily said, which meant she approved of my tactics. "The drawer beside the sink."

I nodded, trying to look confident. "The maid of honor is *on it*."

"What if there's a woman in there with him?" Emily said. "What if that's why he's not answering the door?"

Oh God, no. Please no. Confidence, Lauren. "If there's a woman, then I'll kick her out."

"Seriously?" Kate was watching the back and forth between Emily and me. She had pretty red hair—Sunset Auburn, I knew because she got it done at my salon—that was in loose curls over her shoulders. It went perfectly with the dark green dress we were all wearing as bridesmaids. She was Ryan Riggs' girlfriend, formerly his nanny, and he was nuts about her. "You guys think he has some random in the guest house while his brother is getting married?"

I had no idea. I didn't know who Dex slept with, or how

often. What kind of woman he liked. Whatever his type was, it wasn't good-girl cop's daughters like me.

And yes, Dex was capable of having a random on his brother's wedding day. You never knew *what* Dex would do, especially if it involved making trouble, pissing off his brothers, or both.

But I would brave it. I was two minutes older than Emily, the big sister, and I was the maid of honor.

I put my heels on and walked downstairs to the kitchen. In the living room and the front room of the house, I could hear talking and laughter. The guests were gathering inside, waiting for the cue to go assemble for the ceremony. It was Thanksgiving weekend in Michigan, which meant it was cold and bleak outside, a few tiny flakes of early snow in the air. The ceremony would be held outside, but everyone would go out at the last minute, then come straight back in when it was over. We were Michiganers. We could deal with a little cold.

I opened the drawer beside the sink and rifled through the junk in there. Elastic bands, coins, plastic take-out forks. I had found the key on its key ring when I was approached by a gorgeous man in a suit.

This was Luke Riggs, one of Dex's brothers and Emily's husband-to-be. He was dark-haired and broody and had muscles everywhere under the suit. "What are you doing?" he asked in that lazy drawl that had put girls' panties on the floor all through high school. Including, apparently, my sister's.

"I'm going to get Dex," I told him.

He looked startled. "You mean get him from the guest house?"

"Since that's where he is, yes."

"You better let me do it."

"No. You're the groom, Luke. Stay here."

He winced. "Seriously, Lauren. We don't know what's in there. It might be... bad."

"I'm aware. But Dex is not a nuclear bomb. Whatever is in there, I can take it."

"Is Emily upset? If so, I'll kick his ass myself."

I silently gritted my teeth. This was my life now. I was truly happy that Emily was in love—I really was. I was happy that she had a hot guy who adored her, who had apparently secretly adored her all this time. I was happy that she was having nonstop, smoking-hot, paint-peeling sex with Luke Riggs. I was happy that she showed up to work at our hair salon half the time with a dreamy, over-orgasmed look on her face. I was happy about all of that.

But having my sister and Luke so crazy in love, right in front of my face while I went through a divorce from the man I'd been with since I was seventeen... it made me a teeny, tiny bit miserable. It made me feel like the misfit, the third wheel. I wasn't even dating anyone; the divorce was too raw. I was a dried-up spinster at twenty-six, and it made me jealous and petty and low.

I didn't act jealous or petty or low. That would have made me an asshole. But a small part of me wanted to.

"Emily is fine," I said, answering his question. "It's me that's losing it."

I looked up to see Luke grinning at me. "Don't look so afraid. It's just Dex. You've known him since we were what, sixteen?"

"Fifteen," I said, and sighed. "Okay, wish me luck. Here I go."

"You're a strong, brave woman, Lauren," Luke said, saluting me.

No, I'm not. I'm an empty shell, and I'm miserable, and I have no idea how to fix it. "I know," I said to Luke, and left.

I had grabbed my wrap, and I pulled it around my shoulders as I walked out the back door into the cold. The wrap was soft cashmere and dark chocolate brown, and it perfectly set off the dark green of the dress. All four of us bridesmaids had one. We'd need it to stand by the altar in the cold. I loved mine, and I was probably going to sleep with it all winter. Since I had no human to sleep with, of course. Maybe I'd get a cat.

Divorced women got cats, right? Especially divorced women who—

No. I wasn't going to think about that right now.

I banged the side of my fist on the guest house door, glancing at the darkened windows. "Dex!" I shouted. "It's Lauren. I'm coming in."

No answer. Maybe a faint groan—or maybe that was the wind.

For the first time, I felt a shiver of real alarm. What if something bad had actually happened to Dex while we were all sitting around thinking he was an asshole? Without knocking again, I put my key in the lock and opened the door.

It was quiet and dark in here. With the blinds down and the sky outside overcast, the guest house was suffused with soft gray light. It was a cozy, open space, with a small kitchen to the left of the door and a bachelor bedroom to the right. Empty beer bottles lined the kitchen counter. On the small table was a baggie of weed and the remnants of a few joints. There was the faint, sweet smell of weed in the air, as if it had been smoked hours ago.

There were two suitcases stacked in a corner, one of them open and spilling clothes. *Was that all Dex brought with him from Detroit?* I wondered. *Is that all he owns?* I thought I'd pared my belongings down in a big way after the divorce, but I still had a small condo full of stuff.

In the main room was a bed, messy and piled with sheets and blankets. On the bed was Dex.

He wasn't dead. He was very much alive—and naked.

Not that I could see everything. He was lying on his stomach, and the sheet was pulled carelessly over his ass. But I could see that the rest of him was bare, and beneath the edge of the sheet I could see the unbroken line of bare skin along his hip, which meant he wasn't wearing underwear. He wasn't wearing anything.

I peeled my gaze away from that strip of skin and took in the rest of him. I'd never seen Dex naked—I'd never seen any real-life man naked except for my ex-husband, a fact that I used to be proud of but now made me feel like a loser. The Riggs brothers were all different—Luke had all those bad-boy muscles, Jace was big and powerful, and Ryan was flat-out gorgeous with an athlete's grace. Dex was tall and his body was lean and hard, tight with muscle, the dip of his spine and the line of his shoulders like a well-oiled machine. His legs were lean and perfect, and his biceps were tight and powerful. Something about him reminded me of the MMA fighters you see on cable—a body honed and made for fighting. Except now it was at rest, the muscles lax, the limbs thrown carelessly in the sheets. My gaze traveled to where a single tattoo was inked on his right shoulder, the only tattoo I could see. It was three words, stark against his skin: *Have No Fear.*

I stood there blinking, taking all of it in. For as long as I'd known him, Dex had one kind of wardrobe: battered jeans, worn-out tees, button-downs so well-used that the cuffs were thinning. He kept his hair messy and usually had a scruff of negligent beard on his jaw. It made him look like he'd just gotten off an all-night Greyhound, but now I realized that Dex's clothes were camouflage. Underneath them, he was honed and freaking gorgeous.

I remembered his biceps in the black tee he'd worn the night of the party. The leanness of his body under the thin cotton. The bruise on his neck that I'd thought was a smear of ink.

Dex was a fighter.

I was still standing there speechless when he shifted in the bed and rolled over onto his back. He absently grabbed the sheet as he did so, adjusting it over his crotch. His eyes opened halfway and he blinked at me. He didn't seem in the least surprised to see me.

My eyes caught his and I hesitated.

That was all the opening he needed. Looking more awake now, Dex scrubbed a hand through his hair and smiled. "Morning, Lauren," he said. "Did you come here to kiss me again?"

TWO

Dex

LAUREN PARKER IN MY BEDROOM. Well, well.

Fuck, she looked good. Of course she did. She always looked good, and today she was dressed up. Her honey-blonde hair was swept up from her neck and she wore a dark green dress over her elegant, perfect curves. I took one look at her and made a mental map, a plan of attack. I'd get rid of the wrap first, then unzip the dress. The hair likely had pins in it that I could pull out. The bra —Lauren was 36C or I'd eat my fucking wallet—was likely strapless, clasped at the back. One flick and it would be gone.

The panties were harder to predict. As much as I liked to picture Lauren in a flimsy G-string, she probably wasn't wearing one. I put my money on black, comfortable, full coverage, and it was even possible there was Spanx under there. If there was, it would take me a few extra seconds to get them off. But even with the delay, Operation Get Lauren Naked would take sixty seconds, max.

Her expression told me that Operation Get Lauren Naked was never happening.

"Get out of bed," she snapped. "And *you* kissed *me*."

Yes, I definitely had. "I knew you remembered."

Her cheekbones went red. "Vaguely," she said. "But you know what I really remembered? That Luke and Emily are getting married. Today."

I sighed. The fucking wedding. The last thing I wanted to do today, or ever, was watch my crazy-in-love brother marry his gorgeous fiancée at his fucking wedding. "When is it?" I asked.

"Are you serious?" When I didn't answer, which meant yes, she said, "It's in ninety minutes." She looked at her phone. "No, eighty minutes."

I groaned and scrubbed a hand over my face. Jesus, I'd slept late. The insomnia never fucking quit. "I can't believe Luke made me the best man."

"He was trying to torture you," Lauren said, which was true.

"It's working." I had no interest in weddings—Luke's, or anyone's. I didn't understand them. I'd never met a woman who could stand me for longer than a few weeks without wanting to smash my head in with whatever was handy, let alone fucking marry me. The thought just didn't compute. "Tell everyone I'm sick," I said.

"No," Lauren said.

I dropped the hand that was rubbing my face and looked at her. Her gaze was on my chest and my stomach, but it quickly snapped to my eyes. I looked pretty good, but mostly because I ran my insomnia and anxiety off every day and I barely ate. Being consumed with failure had melted my body fat. Lucky me.

"Seriously," I said to her. "The wedding happens with or without me. Just tell them I'm hung over."

"Are you?" she asked, her gray eyes fixed on mine.

"Not really." I hadn't chosen alcohol to try and kill the sleep-lessness last night. Last night's weapon was weed.

"Then no," Lauren said. She pressed her lips together. "You are doing this, Dex Riggs. You will *not* ruin my sister's wedding."

She was being bossy. Bitchy, even. I'm a nice guy—shut up—but I do not follow rules. Not now. Not ever. There is no one, and I mean no one, who tells me what to do.

I should have told her to fuck off, and take her wedding with her. I even thought about doing it. Put the words together in my head.

Instead I raised my hand and made a circle with my fingertip. "Turn around, Parker."

"Why?"

"Because I'm naked, and in a second you're going to see my dick."

She spun so fast the tendrils of hair lifted off her neck.

I pushed the sheet off me and put my feet on the floor. "I thought you got married," I said to her, standing up and looking at the elegant line of her back. "You've seen one before. It isn't going to bite you."

"Shut up and go take a shower," she said.

I walked off to the bathroom. I took my time. By the time I closed the door behind me, I was laughing.

THREE

Dex

"I DON'T KNOW how you do it," my brother Jace said to me in our place next to the altar. I had gotten here with minutes to spare, but I had gotten here. Thanks to Lauren Parker, I was showered, cleaned up, and suited up. My shoes were shined, my beard was trimmed, my parts were covered, and my breath was minty. This was as good as Dex Riggs ever fucking got.

"Do what?" I said as Emily came down the aisle on her dad's arm. She looked beautiful, I had to admit. I glanced across the altar at Lauren. She was watching Emily, and the look on her face was torn between happiness and pain.

Happiness that her sister was getting married. Pain over her own marriage ending. She was so easy to read. At least for me.

"Piss everyone off," Jace said, answering my question in a whisper. He was a big guy, Jace. Tall and strong. An ex-con who had done time for stealing cars while informing on our father's stolen car operation. Now he was out and living with the woman who was his former counselor, who he was pretty much nuts for. He'd probably marry her, too. "You can make everyone mad by not doing anything."

Emily reached the front, her dad kissed her, and she took Luke's hand. The justice of the peace started talking. Cherish each other forever, something something. Weddings were not for me.

"Bullshit," I whispered to Jace. "No one would have cared if I didn't show up."

"You're hopeless," he said.

I shrugged. I had never claimed otherwise. "I have two joints in the pocket of this suit, and the second this is over, I'm going to smoke both of them."

I felt the heat of a gaze, and found Lauren Parker glaring at me across the altar, her eyes narrowed. She'd probably heard me. Well, too bad. She'd made me put the suit on, but she'd never checked whether I put anything in the pockets.

If she thought I was going to get through this day without weed, she was out of her fucking mind.

I fixed my gaze on hers and stared back. We stayed like that, eyes locked, staring each other down while the justice of the peace blathered on. *Love and honor each other. A union of the body and the soul.* Her eyes were bluish gray. I wondered if she'd had a union of the body and the soul with her ex, Vic Voorhees. I wondered if she'd ever gotten him out of bed and made him put on a suit. I wondered what a union of the body and the soul even felt like.

The ceremony wasn't very long, because it was cold out here. Emily and Luke said *I do*, the justice of the peace finished up, they kissed, and everyone clapped and went inside.

I walked away from the house and toward the guest house, pulling my phone from my pocket. I'd put it on silent, but it had vibrated throughout the ceremony. I circled around behind the guest house to the rotting old picnic bench back there, reading my texts and pulling a joint from my other pocket. I sat on the table with my feet on the bench, lit up, and scrolled.

One of the guys I knew in town: *Hey man, I know this is a long shot but do you know where I can score some—* Delete.

Ashley, who I only vaguely remembered: *Dex!! R U in town?? Let's hook up?? Call me!* Delete.

One of my former colleagues on the Detroit PD: *Looks like the IRS is doing another audit. Buckle up!*

I stared at that one for a long time, the weed warring with the anxiety in my head. It was code, of course—the IRS wasn't doing a fucking audit. He meant that Internal Affairs was taking another look at the incident that had pushed me off the force. The incident that had ended my career as a cop.

No one had ever thought that Dex Riggs would become a cop after high school, least of all my dirtbag father. That was the main reason I did it. I'd had no business being a cop—I didn't have discipline or morality or a willingness to follow rules. I'd only had a chip on my shoulder and a determination to do whatever would make my father hate me even more than he already did.

That, at least, I'd succeeded in. I'd visited my father exactly once in prison, and his hate for me had come off him like a smell. But I hadn't lasted as a cop. I knew that everyone speculated about why. I didn't bother telling anyone the truth.

Looks like the IRS is doing another audit. Buckle up!

I took another hit of the joint and felt some of the panic recede. I caught sight of my hand as I put the last of it out. Two knuckles broken and healed on my right hand, and the fourth finger of my left had never gone straight after a drug dealer broke it with the heel of his boot. All injuries I got on the job. And those were just the bones my own father hadn't broken.

"Hey," a voice said.

I looked up. Lauren was coming toward me, her wrap pulled around her shoulders, her green dress flowing against her long legs. She was carrying two stemmed glasses with champagne in them.

I thought she'd charge in and give me shit, but she said, "Do you want one of these?"

I shrugged and took one. "Sure."

"Everyone's wondering where you are," she said. "They want to do a toast."

I took a sip of the champagne. "I didn't go far."

For a second Lauren looked uncertain, as if she was considering coercing me back into the house. Then she sighed and came to the picnic table. She sat next to me, getting comfortable, putting her high-heeled feet on the seat.

"You'll wreck your dress," I said.

"It'll clean," she replied, and took a big swig of champagne.

I watched her swallow it, then another. Even when she was gulping champagne, I wondered if there was ever a girl as beautiful as Lauren Parker. She was even better looking than she'd been at sixteen.

"They're doing that thing," she said when she put her empty glass down. "That thing where they toast and make the bride and groom kiss."

"Oh, Jesus," I said. "Hold this." I handed her my glass and dug in my pockets, getting out my second joint and my lighter.

When I had it together, I looked over and saw that my glass had been emptied, too. "Is that weed?" Lauren asked, putting the glass down. "Isn't that still illegal? I have no idea."

"Are you fucking serious?" I said. I put the joint between my lips and lit it. "Call the cops and ask them."

"I don't have to call the cops, Dex. My mother is one. She's right over there." She pointed back toward the house.

I ignored that. If Nora Parker wanted me in jail, she could come out here and get me. "Want some?" I asked Lauren.

"I don't—"

"Or do you really want to go back in the house and sit through that reception?"

Lauren's jaw set in misery, and her gray eyes met mine. "Give me that."

She took the joint. It was either the first hit she'd ever done or damned close, but she didn't do too badly. She held her breath and exhaled a plume of smoke, making even that seem elegant. "How many more of these weddings will we have to go to?" she asked, handing the joint back to me.

"Two at least," I said, taking a hit myself. "Jace and Ryan are next. Don't throw that dress out."

Lauren groaned. "Two more weddings where I get to be the single loser, cheering on the happy couple."

"At least neither of them will ask me to be the best man." I'd made sure of that by taking my brothers out to a hand job place for Luke's bachelor party. They'd rebelled, and I'd ended up fist-fighting Ryan in the parking lot. He had a pretty good punch, but then again so did I. "How do you feel?" I asked her.

"My face is a little numb." She touched her fingertips to her cheek. I watched her frown, then blink. Trying to figure out exactly how she felt. Her face was so expressive.

"That's how you know it's working," I said. "Relax. It'll wear off in thirty minutes, tops."

"I kind of like it," she said. "I'm not so upset anymore. It's like it doesn't matter."

"You've just discovered the beauty of weed," I said. "Now I've corrupted you. It's all downhill from here."

That made her smile. I blinked, filing that image away. "You corrupted me ten years ago," she said.

"No, I didn't. I kissed you. That isn't the same thing." I took another hit of the joint, then ground it out, unwilling to think about that night. I had no idea why that memory was so painful.

No, that was a lie. I knew exactly why.

And because I'm a glutton for punishment, because I can't leave the most painful things alone, I said to her, "Vic Voorhees, Parker? Really?"

At the mention of her ex's name, the smile dropped from her face. She looked sad again, and I wished I could eat my words. Neither of us needed to dig up this old news.

Except it bothered me that Lauren Parker had kissed me—really kissed me—and less than a month later she was dating Vic Voorhees. They were inseparable for the rest of high school. And then she went and married him.

The best girl who ever kissed me got fucking *married*.

For sure, I had kicked her out of my house right after I kissed her. But that was for her own good, because the cops were coming. I had meant to make it up to her. I had meant to maybe even give it a shot. But I didn't have time, because before I could talk to her again she was Vic Voorhees' girlfriend.

I should have known better than to think I deserved a single fucking thing. It was a lesson I learned the hard way.

"Dex," she said now, her voice heavy in a way I'd never heard before, "I don't think I want to talk about it. About me and Vic."

On second thought I didn't want to hear it either. "Yeah, you're right."

"I mean, you kissed me, but it was the middle of a party, right? It was just a kiss. It didn't mean anything. And then Vic asked me out, and he was a nice guy. I'd never had a boyfriend before." She sighed. "I suppose you guessed that part."

Jesus. "Forget I said anything."

"Getting divorced sucks," she said, ignoring me. "Don't ever get divorced, Dex. I mean it."

"Yeah, okay, look—"

"We broke up because we couldn't have a baby."

The words hung there in the cold air between us.

Strangely, they hurt. They hurt because I pictured her trying to make a baby with that fucking guy who didn't deserve her. But they hurt worse because of the look on her face. Like the fact she didn't have a baby had broken her heart.

Not just broken it. Torn it into tiny bloody chunks. For a second I could see everything about Lauren, and she was a walking open wound. Everyone thought she was fine and she wasn't. How did everyone not see it?

It was too harsh, that moment. Too raw. I wished more than anything that I had another joint to smoke, but I didn't. Instead I used one of my other weapons and lightened the mood. "I'm not surprised Vic couldn't get the job done," I said. "His sperm were probably asleep."

The corners of her eyes crinkled, though she didn't quite smile. Some of the heaviness lifted. "Dex," she said.

"Come on, admit it. The guy is walking Ambien."

Amused now. "He is not."

"Sure he is. He was dull in high school and I bet he's dull now. No woman ever looks at VapoRub and thinks, 'That guy can knock me up.'"

"Don't call him that." But the words had no heat to them. We'd all called Vic VapoRub in high school, and it had driven him fucking nuts. Which of course meant we kept doing it. It was by far the most interesting thing about him.

"Now, me," I said, "I could do it in a heartbeat. You're probably pregnant right now just from seeing me naked earlier."

She laughed outright at that, her cheeks going red. "I didn't see you naked. Just mostly naked."

"Thank God. If you'd seen the whole thing, you'd be having twins." I pointed to the narrow valley of space between us. "I probably knocked you up by sitting next to you on this bench. You're welcome."

"Stop it!" She was laughing now. *I made her laugh,* I thought, amazed. Then I wondered what I would do to make her laugh again.

Anything. Fucking anything.

I slid off the bench and stood up. "You should probably go back inside," I said. "It's cold out here." Because I had to. It was the same pattern as the party ten years ago. There was no good reason for Lauren to get close to me.

Her laugh trailed off. "You're probably right." She scooted forward on the table, and I held out a hand. She took it and stood, using me to keep her balance on her heels. "As much as I'd like to, I can't avoid my responsibilities forever."

"You can get pretty close," I said.

Lauren looked at me. "I don't think you believe that. Come back inside with me."

I shook my head. "Not happening."

She glanced down, and we both realized I still held her hand in mine. She let go of me—a little reluctantly, I thought. Then again, maybe it was the weed and the champagne.

"What are you going to do?" she asked.

I shrugged. "Change out of this suit. Get out of here." I looked around. "I think I might go for a drive."

"That's it?"

No, that wasn't it. I'd drink—alone. I'd brood over what I'd been texted about the IAD investigation. And maybe I'd run into a woman for a random hookup—though, looking at Lauren right now, I wasn't in the mood.

She's out of your league, idiot.

"Don't worry about me, Parker," I said to her. "I'll be fine."

She shook her head, as if she didn't believe me. Then she turned and walked away.

FOUR

One month later – Christmas Eve
Lauren

AS A BORN and bred Michigan girl, I was very familiar with winter. Snow was as much a part of my life as summer barbecues or fall leaves. So I was dressed for the cold. The problem was, I wasn't dressed for the cold of sitting in my freezing car in a near-empty parking lot, turning the key over and over and getting nothing.

"Shit," I said, my breath frosting in the air in front of me. It was three o'clock in the afternoon on Christmas Eve, and the sky was already getting ominously dark. It looked like snow was on the way.

I looked around. The lot was nearly empty and getting emptier by the minute. The building I had been in had closed as soon as I left, and everyone was going home. Everyone except me.

I flipped the tops of my mittens open and picked up my

phone with my fingerless gloves. The mitten-fingerless glove combo was the best thing ever invented; I had three pairs, because Michigan. This pair was lavender colored and soft, matching the hat I had pulled over my ears. I woke up my phone and flipped through the numbers in my address book.

I could try to flag down a stranger and ask for a jump, which was unlikely to be successful as well as a great way to get murdered. I could call a roadside assistance service. But my brother-in-law ran Riggs Auto, and if I called a roadside service and paid their exorbitant price, I would never hear the end of it.

But I couldn't call Luke. Because he'd come get me, and then he'd see the building behind me, the one I was coming from.

No. Just no.

The one person—the *only* person—who could help me in this particular situation was Dex Riggs. For reasons. And I didn't have his number.

I hadn't seen Dex since the wedding, when he'd managed to cheer me out of my self-pitying slump. I knew he was still living in the guest house behind Emily and Luke's place, and I knew he was working with Ryan at the second location of Riggs Auto, which the boys called Riggs Auto Two. I looked up the number on my phone and dialed it.

"Riggs Auto," the man answered on the other end. Damn. I'd gotten Ryan, not Dex.

"Ryan," I said, trying to sound casual. "It's Lauren. Is Dex there?"

"Lauren?" he said, obviously surprised. "Um, sure. Good thing you caught us, we were about to close. Hold on."

A few rustles, and then Dex's distinct low voice came on the line. "Yeah?"

"Hi," I said. "It's Lauren. I'm stuck in a parking lot and my car won't start."

The briefest pause, in which I knew I'd surprised him. "You okay?"

"Yes. I know it's weird. But it has to be you who helps me. Only you. You'll understand when you get here."

Another brief pause. This was Dex's day for surprises. Then: "Tell me where."

I gave him the address.

"You got somewhere to get warm?"

"I'm fine," I said. "There's a plaza a few minutes' walk from here if I need it. But can I ask you something? Please don't tell anyone you're coming to get me. Not Ryan, not anyone."

"That so?" Dex said. The brief answers, I knew, meant that Ryan was in earshot somewhere.

"I know it's weird, it's just... I don't want anyone to know where I am. Please."

"Fine," he said. "Later, Parker." He hung up.

I blew out a breath, watching it plume. The last car drove out of the lot; it was just me now. My feet were getting cold and my fingers were starting to sting. I was going to flip my mittens closed again when my phone rang.

It was Emily. If I didn't answer, she'd hit redial and then she'd panic. So I answered.

"Lauren, it's Christmas Eve," Em said. "Come to the house."

I kicked my feet, trying to get the circulation going in my chilled toes. "We've been over this, Em. This is your first Christmas as a married couple. Go and do the cozy romantic thing."

"But you're all alone," she argued.

Ah, yes, the refrain of the happily coupled person to the sad single person. *You're all alone! No one can possibly be happy alone!* I was going to get this every Christmas, every birthday, for eternity.

This was the road I'd chosen when I asked Vic for a divorce. And even though it had its shitty side, I still didn't regret it.

"I'm fine." How many times had I said that? Twice in the last five minutes. *I'm fine*. It would probably be etched on my gravestone. *I'm fine*.

"Mom says she invited you over and you said no."

"True. Dad invited me, too." Our parents had surprised us earlier in the year by getting amicably divorced, which made Christmas even weirder. Our father now lived in a small rental apartment, surrounded by the bare necessities and not much else. "It was just a pity invite from Dad, because he was going bowling anyway with the new bowling league he joined. Everyone should stop worrying about me. I have a nice condo and lots of work to do."

"You can't work on Christmas Eve, you dork. No one is working."

"Actually, it's the perfect time to catch up." After handing over the day-to-day reins of the salon to Emily, I had spent time coaching Ryan's girlfriend, Kate, on the startup of her tutoring business. I'd enjoyed it so much that I had started doing consulting work for other people who wanted to start small businesses, teaching them the ins and outs of loans, accounting, taxes, and business plans. I was good at it, I enjoyed it, and most importantly it was helping to heal the burnout I'd had from running the salon.

I loved The Big Do. It was my baby. But I'd done fourteen-hour days for too many years, and lately, especially with the divorce, I hadn't been able to handle it alone. Enter Emily.

"Lauren, you're being lame," my sister said. "Unless you're lying about sitting at home on Christmas Eve. Are you lying?"

"Maybe. Maybe I joined Dad's bowling league."

"Ugh, shut up. You're too hot to join an old divorced guys' bowling league. I seriously need to work on you."

A car pulled into the empty parking lot. A beat-up dark blue Mustang with white racing stripes on the hood. It made a godawful noise, as if a muffler had never graced the car with its presence in its long life. It barreled through the wet snow toward me with a roar.

"Um," I said to Emily, "I have to go."

"Where are you right now? I can hear something in the background."

The car pulled up to mine, its front bumper inches from my own front bumper. The door opened and Dex got out.

"I'm out," I said into the phone.

"Alone?"

I watched Dex through the windshield. Worn jeans, black boots, unzipped black winter coat, hoodie that said DETROIT PD. He had a trim dark beard and his longish dark hair was tangling in the wind. He walked through the snow toward my window.

"No," I said to Emily. "Not alone."

"With who, then?"

"I'll call you later," I said, and hung up.

Dex opened my driver's door and leaned in, one long forearm draped on the roof of my car. "Parker," he said. "I told you to get warm."

"I'm not that cold," I argued, though my teeth were trying to chatter.

He stood back. "Sit in my car while I get this done."

I walked on frozen feet through the snow and sunk happily into the passenger seat of his warmed-up car. The leather seats were deep and new and the entire space smelled like man and Dex. I watched him go back and forth, opening both hoods and getting out his jumper cables.

It was the simplest operation, but it still gave me little shivers to watch. Call it competence porn. My ex had no idea how to jump a battery. He would have called roadside assistance by now and already given his credit card.

When he had connected the cables, Dex opened the driver's door and got into his car next to me. He started the car. "You leave your lights on?" he asked me.

"I've never done that in my life."

He nodded, not questioning it. "You might need a new battery, then. I can hook you up." He pointed through the window at the building. "That's why you wanted this top secret?"

I looked where he was pointing, though I already knew what he was looking at. It was a fertility clinic. I'd been the last appointment of the day. "Yes. If I called Luke to come get me, he'd tell Emily where I was. And Em means well, but she'd tell my mother. My father. Everyone." I looked away, out my window. "I can't handle that right now."

"I get that," Dex said. "Are you getting a treatment or something?"

"You could say that, I guess. It's a sperm bank."

I found myself bracing—for laughter, for criticism. For pain. But all he said was, "Jesus," his voice soft.

"What does that mean?" My voice was harsh; my defenses were up. I couldn't help it. "Just say it, Dex."

My hostility had no effect on him. He ran a hand through his hair. "It means it's Christmas Eve, and you want a baby so much you're willing to get some stranger's junk."

"It was just a preliminary appointment." I already had a second appointment booked right after New Year's, but I didn't tell him that. "And they don't refer to it as 'junk,' by the way."

"Calm down, Parker. I'm not insulting you." He held out his hand, palm up. "Give me your key."

I put my car key in his hand, and he got out of the car again. The wind had kicked up now, making his hair blow as he walked to my car. He got in, and a second later I heard the happy sound of my car starting.

He left it running, disconnected the cables, and closed the hoods. Then he got back in his car with me. I should have gotten out, I realized. Gone to my own car, thanked him, and driven away. But I hadn't moved.

Moving meant I had to get out and go home. Alone.

Or maybe join a bowling league. Neither one had any appeal.

Dex got back in next to me. We sat there for a moment, neither of us speaking, the warm car running, the wind blowing outside. He seemed as reluctant to leave as I was.

We weren't looking at each other, weren't touching, and the electricity still sparked between us. He had always done this to me. Five minutes with Dex Riggs, doing something as mundane as jumping my car, and I felt more alive than I had in weeks.

"Luke invited me over tonight," he said finally, breaking the quiet. "A pity invite."

"Same here," I said. "My invite was from Emily."

"This is how it's going be, right?"

"Yes, it is."

"Do you have anywhere else to go?" he asked me.

With Dex, I told the truth. "No. Nowhere."

He looked away, ran a hand through his hair again. "Are you really going to try and get pregnant with a stranger's junk?"

"Probably, yes."

"But you haven't yet. So you're not pregnant now."

"No, I'm not."

He nodded. "Good," he said. "Go get in your car, Parker, and follow me. Let's go drink."

FIVE

Dex

I TOOK her to a place called Malone's, which was a hole in the wall that served beer, a few kinds of pub food, and not much else. It sucked, but it was on the outskirts of town and it was frequented by losers. I knew we wouldn't see anyone we knew. I also knew that it would be open, because just like me, the losers would have nowhere else to go.

I got us a booth and a few beers. Lauren pulled off her hat and her mittens, her nose and her cheeks red, her honey-blonde hair a tousled mess. She produced a hair elastic from her pocket and swiped her hair up off her neck, tying it back with a few quick flicks of her wrists. I never had any idea how the hell women did that.

"I like this," she said of the shitty bar. "We won't see anyone we know."

"Settle in," I said.

"Are you a regular here?"

"No."

"Are you a regular anywhere?"

"No."

Lauren waggled her eyebrows. "Dex Riggs, the mysterious loner."

"Something like that." I sipped my beer. I tried to feel my usual empty bitterness, but she was so fucking pretty. Jesus. "Tell me why you decided to go to a sperm bank on Christmas Eve."

She sipped her beer and shook her head, swallowing. "I don't want to talk about me. I get to ask the questions first."

"Like what?"

She thought it over, as if she had so many questions for me that she found it hard to pick one. "Why did you move back to Westlake?" she asked.

And just like that, my defenses went up. I had a list of tactics for questions like this. Deflect; make a joke, preferably crude; insult the other person; if necessary, leave. Actually answering was not on the list.

But to Lauren I said, "Because I flunked out of being a cop."

"Is that true?" she asked. "I've heard the rumors, but I have a hard time believing them."

"Why?"

"Because people are full of shit."

Lauren fucking Parker. Honest to God. "I quit the force," I said. "That part is true."

She sipped her beer again. "Were you corrupt?" she asked as if we were talking about the weather. "You can tell me. I've grown up around cops all my life. There were corrupt cops on the Westlake PD until a few months ago."

I thought of the text I had on my phone. *Buckle up!* I rubbed the short beard on my jaw. "The answer to that is complicated."

"I don't think you were," she said. "But for some reason you're okay with people thinking you were. Why is that?"

Jesus. "Can we change the subject?"

"Fine. You quit the force. But why come back here? I thought you Riggs boys all hated Westlake."

"We did. We do." I thought it over. My brothers and I had all hated this place growing up, yet now, years later, we were all back here. "It's different with our father in prison. This way we don't have to look at him."

Lauren didn't flinch. My father, that piece of shit, was serving time right now for running a stolen car ring through Riggs Auto and trying to run over one of his shady business partners when they disagreed. Everyone knew it. "Okay," she said, "but what if he gets out and comes home?"

"He isn't getting out," I said.

"Ever?"

"Ever."

"I didn't think he had a life sentence." She paused, looked at my face. "Dex. What did you do?"

"Nothing," I said, sipping my beer. "Almost nothing. It's better if you don't know. But trust me, my father is not getting out of prison." What's the point of knowing a wide circle of dirtbag cops and criminals if you can't get them to help you out every once in a while?

Lauren was still looking at me carefully. "You hate him."

"I very much fucking do, yes."

"Why?"

"You need to ask me that?"

She swallowed, and I followed the motion in her slender throat. "The night you kissed me, you had a bruise on your neck. You said you walked into a door."

I said nothing.

"Did he hit all four of you?" she asked after a moment.

"Yes. Me more than the others, but everyone got a share sooner or later." I watched a drop of condensation move down the side of my beer glass and touched it with my thumb. I was the oldest and Dad's most hated, so I got smacked around the most. Sometimes I took it so my brothers wouldn't, which was fine with me. A hit was a hit, so what did it matter?

"I'm sorry, Dex," Lauren said.

I shrugged. It was ancient history now; Dad had stopped hitting me after the first few times I hit him back. "Mostly he drove our mothers away, then left us all to fend for ourselves like animals. We had to fight through every day. My brothers could have been different, had different lives, if it wasn't for him." I leaned back in my seat. "My brothers might forgive him or make their peace. That's up to them. But I never will. Not ever. So no, he is never coming home on my watch."

She leaned back in her own seat, her face serious. "Damn it. I don't know what to say."

I hadn't meant to bring her down, honestly. She had enough on her plate. "This is too heavy," I said. "Tell me, how easy is it to walk into a sperm bank and get some guy's jizz?"

"Pretty easy," Lauren said. "The first appointment is just to go over things and decide what kind of donor I want."

I put my glass down. "What kind of donor?"

"Yes. Height, race, education level. Eye color, hair color. They have profiles of the men, and the consultant goes through it with you." She took a sip of her beer. "Then we talk about how to implant the sperm. What kind of procedure to use. Whether I should do it at home or have the doctor do it."

It took a lot to shock me, but that did it. I'd never thought about any of that before. Of course not—you had to want kids to think about it. Which usually meant you had a serious girlfriend, something I'd never had. The idea of any of the women I'd dated having a kid was sort of horrifying. "That sounds complicated," I said. "You know I could just help you out, right?"

Lauren put her glass down, her cheeks flushing and her jaw going tight. "Dex."

"I'm just saying." I wanted to lighten the mood, but I didn't want her to think I was making fun of her. I gestured to myself. "I've got what you need right here. You've seen the goods mostly naked already. Plus you already know my height, race, and hair color."

She shook her head. Her expression wavered between annoyed, amused, and maybe a little turned on. "You're being an ass."

"You really want to get knocked up by a tube on a doctor's table? Come on, Parker. That sounds fucking awful and you know it."

She pressed her lips together and looked away.

I'd offended her. She was lonely and hurting, and it was Christmas Eve, and I wasn't making it any better. I had a knack for making people feel like shit, but somehow with Lauren I wanted to kick myself. I just hoped she wouldn't dump my drink over my head and leave.

"Look," I said, picking up one of the menus and changing the subject, "we'll get something to eat and talk about something else. Maybe there's—"

"What if I said yes?" she said.

I put the menu down and looked at her.

She was looking at me again. Her cheeks were red, but her chin was up. "What if I said yes?" she said again. "What if I said I wanted to try it? Because you're right. I *don't* want to get pregnant on a doctor's table. I don't want to look at photos and profiles and pick my baby's father. A lot of people do it, which is fine. But I was in the clinic today, and I thought..." She trailed off, as if she couldn't find the words. "What if I took you up on it? Would you do it?"

It was a crazy idea. Insane. I could barely even date a woman for a week, let alone be father material. But I said, "Sure I would."

Her gaze caught mine. "You're being serious."

I leaned forward across the table so she could see me clear. "Parker, I am always fucking serious. You want to get knocked up, I will knock you up. You want a baby, I'll give you one. I'll give it my best shot, at least, and we'll have a lot of fucking fun. What have you got to lose?"

For a second her gray-blue gaze wavered, as if she was thinking it over. Then she seemed to make a decision. The corner of her mouth twitched and her shoulders relaxed. That's when I knew I had won.

"Okay, Riggs," she said. "I'll give you a shot. You're on."

SIX

Lauren

"IT ISN'T AS simple as you think," I said to Dex. "There are rules."

We were on our second beer. The wind had picked up outside, blowing flakes of snow against the bar window. Even though it was Christmas Eve, the loners in this bar showed no signs of going home, wherever home was. Dex and I fit right in.

"It is simple," Dex said. "We get out of here and I knock you up."

I was trying to play it casual, but my cheeks went hot. Again. The fact was, sitting across from him like this was getting me bothered. I could see the dip of his clavicle where his hoodie was unzipped, and I kept staring at the perfect line of his shoulders. The short, trimmed beard on his jaw. Those damn cheekbones and those dark blue eyes. Dex Riggs, when he was being sincere for once, was an overload of sexiness.

But no—I had *not* suggested this purely because I wanted to sleep with him. I mean, I didn't want to sleep with him. He was a means to an end.

And still, my brain kept flashing back to what he'd looked like sprawled in bed, mostly naked. The landscape of muscles in his back. The tattoo on his shoulder. *Have No Fear.* If everything went as planned, I'd be seeing it up close.

I'd feel all of him up close.

A means to an end. Right.

I could be strong here. "It isn't exactly that simple," I insisted. "We could have sex right now, tonight, and it wouldn't work."

"Fine then," Dex said easily. "We'll call it practice."

There I went, all hot and bothered again. I tried not to squirm in my seat. "I don't think either of us needs practice, Dex. That part is easy."

"I know you," he said, sipping his beer. "I'm willing to bet a thousand dollars you've never been with anyone but Vic Voorhees."

"I'm not taking that bet, because you're right."

"Then you need practice, Lauren. Trust me."

I felt that shiver straight down between my legs, and at first I didn't know why. Then I realized it was because he had called me Lauren instead of Parker. I cleared my throat. "Okay, well, aside from insulting my ex, let's move on. I don't need practice, and I'm not fertile right now. So you're not getting laid tonight."

He smiled a little, that bad-boy smirk. "You mean *you're* not getting laid."

"I'm used to it." The words were out of my mouth before I could think, and I wished I could call them back, but Dex only kept smiling and made no comment.

I dug in my purse for my phone. "If you want to do this, the first step is that we both get tested. When the test results are in, we can start."

Dex frowned, but agreed. "Fine."

"Give me your number," I said. When he dictated it, I sent him a text. I heard his phone buzz in his back pocket.

"What is that?" he asked me.

"My schedule," I said. When he looked blank, I clarified: "My ovulation schedule."

His eyebrows went up.

"Based on when I finished my last period, we have six days before I'm fertile again. That puts us between Christmas and New Year's. It gives us time to get the tests done, but once I'm fertile we'll have to maximize those days."

"Jesus, Parker," Dex said.

"That isn't all," I told him. "Aside from getting the blood test, you have work to do." I pointed to his glass. "That's your last beer, because there will be no drinking during this process. No weed, either."

"What? Why not?"

"Motility." He looked blank again, and I had to remember that he hadn't been living with this nonstop for two years like I had. "Sperm motility, Dex. How fast they swim."

"Hey," he said, offended. "They swim just fine."

"Well, make them swim better. Alcohol and weed are out, cold turkey. Take some Vitamin C supplements. Zinc, too. Eat nutrient-rich food. Do you have any tight underwear?"

"*What?*"

"If you have any, don't wear it. Boxer shorts are best." I had to pause for a second, picturing him in boxer shorts. Sweet lord. "Um, right. Don't ride a bike or sit in a hot tub."

"The fuck?" He ran a hand through his hair. "You have strange rules, Parker. I'm living in the guest house. You think I have a hot tub?"

"Eat a proper diet," I said, ignoring him. "Exercise, but not too much. And for the next six days, until we can get started, don't... er..."

He waited. "Don't what?"

I swallowed. "Don't ejaculate."

We stared at each other for a long moment, the words hanging in the air between us.

"So, you're telling me not to jerk off," Dex said, his voice flat.

"Basically, yes." I licked my lip. "Or, um, have sex. Which brings up the other rule. If this is going to work, then you can't be with anyone else. Until I get pregnant, we're exclusive."

Now he looked annoyed. "You're actually suggesting I would do all of this while I'm banging someone else?"

"I'm just laying out the rules," I said.

"Fine, then, so am I. You don't fuck anyone else either." He leaned forward. "And until we start, you don't get off."

I shook my head. "It doesn't work that way. The biology—"

"I don't give a fuck. Six days, Parker. Until I get my hands on you, you don't come."

I looked into his dark blue eyes and I laughed. "You have no idea how easy that is for me. I've just had a failed IVF treatment, a divorce, and six months single in my hometown with my mother and my sister worrying over every detail of my life. I'm this close to joining my dad's bowling league. My sex drive is somewhere in Tijuana. I don't even remember what an orgasm feels like at this point, or how I'd get one."

He just watched me and let that sit there, let the words I'd spoken sink back into my head. After a minute, he smiled.

I was lying. He knew it; I knew it. The true part was that my sex drive had vanished for longer than I wanted to think about. But sitting right here, looking at Dex... it was back. My skin was flushed warm all over and I could feel my nipples against the fabric of my bra. I could feel every inch of my body. I hadn't felt like this in a long, long time.

And six days felt pretty long all of a sudden. Because after this, when I was home alone in bed tonight, I could think about him and sneak my hand under the covers and...

"Six days," Dex said, as if he was reading my mind. "If I have to do it, then so do you."

"I can do it," I said with a confidence I didn't feel.

"If you do," he said, "in six days I'll knock you up. You've got yourself a deal."

SEVEN

Dex

WE REOPENED Riggs Auto two days after Christmas. The snow was hard and frosty on the ground, the sun bright. The city was sluggish, the way cities are in that nothing Christmas-to-New Year's week—a few people out and about who had no choice, while everyone else stayed home.

We weren't busy, which was good because we were short-staffed at Riggs Auto One. Luke and Emily had taken off on a delayed honeymoon, driving down to Arizona for a week. That left Jace alone at Riggs Auto One, which he didn't mind—Jace was a loner if there ever was one. All of us Riggs brothers were. When you didn't have anyone, you didn't expect anyone.

"You're late," Ryan said when I walked in. He was just busting my balls, because nothing was happening. He was sitting on one of the folding chairs in the shop, his boots up on the messy desk.

I shrugged. "So what?" I unzipped my coat. I was late because I'd gone to get a blood test, of all the fucking crazy things. Because I was apparently going to knock up Lauren Parker in three days.

I hadn't changed my mind, which surprised even me. I hoped she hadn't, either, because I was still in.

I couldn't say why. I just was.

Ryan looked me up and down. "You're not hung over." He squinted harder. "You showered."

"Very observant, fuckface. They teach you that in baseball school?" Ryan was a minor league player until his injured shoulder put him out of the game. Now he lived in Westlake with his girlfriend and his son and he fixed cars with me. He seemed stupidly happy, which usually pissed me off.

"Merry Christmas, Santa Dex," Ryan shot back. It was in our DNA for Ryan and I to trade shots. Our father had knocked up two different women, which meant we were only four months apart. We'd been fighting practically since we were born. It was something of a miracle that we'd run Riggs Auto Two for so long without killing each other.

Ryan swung his feet off the desk and stood up, coming closer. "You don't smell like weed," he said, sniffing.

"It's ten o'clock in the morning." When he looked at me with his eyebrows up, I said, "Jesus. What's your point?"

"I don't know why you're clean and sober this morning, but it's a good thing. Because we have a customer."

I looked around pointedly. "Is that so? I don't see any customers."

"I didn't say customers. I said customer." He picked up a piece of paper from the desk. "We have *the* customer. The only one we need."

I took the paper from him and looked at it. It was a photo from an email, but even printed on our crappy printer I could see what it was. "This is a Porsche. The 924 Carrera GT." It was a classic car, rare. A vintage car lover's wet dream. It was also one of the most expensive Porsches ever made.

"Yes, it is," Ryan said, "and it's coming here. Today. Because we're restoring it."

I looked up from the photo. "What are you talking about?"

"The guy who bought this is rich," Ryan said, pointing at the sheet. "Obviously. He says it needs a lot of work. It doesn't even run. He bought it anyway, because it's his baby. And he wants us to restore it."

"You're kidding me." Aside from doing people's day-to-day repairs, Ryan and I had started doing custom restorations. We were good at finding rare parts and bringing old cars to life again. The restoration customers were fewer, but they paid more. They didn't care that a new car would be cheaper, because they didn't want a new car. They wanted *this* car. So they paid.

We'd done a few good jobs, and we'd started making money. Word had gotten around. But I had no idea we had a job of this kind coming in.

"How much is he paying?" I asked Ryan.

"Whatever it takes," Ryan said. "And he isn't full of shit. He gave us a ten thousand dollar deposit."

"Ten thousand bucks?"

He nodded. "The check already cleared. It's legit, Dex. The tow truck is going to be here any minute."

As if on cue, we heard the rumble of a truck engine outside. Ryan walked to the bay door and hit the button for it to open. Cold air blasted in and I zipped my coat again.

This was huge. Fucking huge. So big it made me nervous. I'd been on a downward slide for so long I didn't know what good luck looked like.

As if on cue, my phone buzzed in my coat pocket. I pulled it out and didn't recognize the number. I answered it anyway. "Yeah?"

"Mr. Dexter Riggs?"

Literally no one called me that, ever. This was going to be bad. "Maybe. What do you want?"

"This is James Blanco from the Detroit PD Internal Affairs Division. I'd like to arrange an interview with you about—"

"You can't talk to me," I said. The garage door was open now, and the tow truck was bringing in the Porsche. Bright red, the paint job a little the worse for wear. It was a goddamned beautiful car. I knew men who would get on their knees and kiss that car's tires.

"Actually, I'm talking to you right now," Blanco said on the phone.

I watched Ryan wave the truck in, then put a hand up to stop it. The driver hopped out to start unhitching.

"You're not talking to me," I said. "I'm not on the force anymore. I'm a private citizen. So we're not talking."

"Actually, Mr. Riggs, I am looking for information about—"

"Get a subpoena," I said, and hung up.

The tow truck driver unhooked that sweet, sweet car. He and Ryan had a conversation, and then the tow truck drove off. Ryan closed the bay door again and turned to me. "Ten thousand dollars," he said, his breath frosting in the cold air. "Let's get started, dickface."

I stood frozen for a minute. There were no words in my throat. I had no illusions that hanging up on that phone call would do anything more than buy me time. A few weeks maybe, since it was the holiday season and a little harder to get a judge's signature on a subpoena. The clock was ticking.

"Well?" Ryan said. "What are you waiting for?"

I cleared my throat. "Fuck you, Babe Ruth," I said to my brother. "Time to get to work."

EIGHT

Lauren

SINCE MY SISTER had finally decided to take a honeymoon with her hot new husband, I was left in charge of the hair salon. Usually Em did the day-to-day management while I did the behind the scenes things: ordering supplies, dealing with the accountant and the bank, issuing paychecks. Except until some-time after New Year's—whenever Em and Luke decided to drive home—all of the jobs were mine.

We'd had a rush in the first few weeks of December, because a lot of women get their hair done before the holidays. We had a second rush this week as the women who were too busy before used their week off to get their hair done for New Year's. The weather was cold and there was a nasty flu going around, so we were short-staffed. Our shipment of manicure supplies was delayed by the holidays. Oh, and every customer was in a hurry, newly broke, and in a shitty mood.

I scrambled through the days the best I could. I swiped credit cards. I took phone calls. I answered complaints. I even shoveled the front walk and poured ice melter over it so no customer would slip, fall, and sue me. At the end of each day I fell into bed exhausted, wondering how I had done this alone for so many years. The entire time I'd started up The Big Do and built it into a business was a blur. How long had I spent doing nothing but work?

The salon made a good profit. That was why I had put my blood, sweat, and tears into it. But I realized now that maybe... just maybe I had put so many hours into work because I didn't have much else in my life. My marriage wasn't very exciting. Vic had a decent job selling insurance and had never shown an interest in helping me with the business. The fact was, even in our early twenties, there had been evenings when Vic had watched football while I fell asleep by nine.

Okay, the truth: That had been *most* evenings.

It was three days to New Year's. I was in the office at the back of the shop, sorting stacks of papers, trying to figure out where to start. It was the first time I'd had more than a few minutes to focus on anything except daily emergencies.

My phone pinged with a text. *Are we still on, Parker?* wrote Dex Riggs.

I paused, my mind temporarily registering nothing but those words. I hadn't heard from Dex since the night we'd made our agreement. I'd half expected him never to mention it again, or to laugh at me if I brought it up. *You were actually serious? Come on, Parker.*

But he was serious. He was in.

I flipped through my phone and checked my calendar, even though I knew my cycle as well as I knew how to spell my own name. *We're on,* I told him. *You have two days to wait.*

There was a pause, and then the dots moved. *Who says?*

A shiver of excitement went straight through my body. Outside, someone in the salon laughed. I was actually standing here in my office, negotiating sex with Westlake's baddest bad boy. An agreement for raunchy, no-strings-attached, *unprotected* sex. Probably lots of it.

Hopefully lots of it.

There's a schedule, I wrote. *I even sent it to you. You know the rules.*

Fuck the rules, Dex wrote back.

Or not, I wrote. *Besides, I don't see your blood test paperwork yet. Or did you decide to overlook that part? No paperwork, Dex, and you don't get anything two days from now. Not even a scrap.*

There. I won that one, I thought. Forceful and confident and even a little bit snarky. I could totally do this.

Outside, the bell over the shop's front door rang. There was a murmur of voices I couldn't quite hear, quietly excited. And then a low, sexy voice I recognized: "I'm here to see your boss."

I walked to the office door and pulled it open. Dex was already striding through the salon, his jeans and black wool coat completely out of place. He was an almost visible wave of testosterone of the kind we never saw in here. Every woman's head turned as he walked by. Two of the stylists had paused with their scissors in the air while the women in the chair craned their necks.

He didn't notice. He was looking at me.

"Lauren," he said, heading straight for me.

My gaze flicked past his shoulder to Georgie, who was watching open-mouthed. She knew who Dex Riggs was. Everyone did—at least, everyone who had gone to Westlake High while the Riggs boys were there. Which was a lot of the people I knew, because Westlake wasn't a very big town.

"Dex," I said, keeping my chin up. "What can I do for you?"

"A word," he said. He put one hand lightly on my waist, backed me into the office, and closed the door behind us.

Oh, shit. Now *everyone* was going to talk.

"What are you doing?" I asked him. It was supposed to be a scolding, but my voice came out breathy and excited instead.

He held up a hand, and for the first time I realized he was holding a few sheets of paper. "Your tests," he said. He stepped forward into my space, backing me against the desk, and dropped the papers on top of my stack. "Here you go, your majesty."

He had brought the cold outside air with him. He smelled like winter and wool and Dex. He was so close I felt like I was sixteen again, backed against the wall at his party. I hadn't moved then, and I didn't move now.

"I'm going to read those results," I told him. "I'll have mine to you this afternoon."

His gaze dropped down my body and he looked at my clothes. Black leggings, boots, a soft sweater that pulled down over my hips. "Whatever," he said, frowning.

He looked good. Like he'd been sleeping. I fought the urge to trace my fingertip along the stupidly perfect line of his jaw. "You haven't been drinking?" I asked him. "No weed?"

His fingertips touched my hips, then moved lightly down to the hem of my sweater. "I said I wouldn't."

My breath hitched as I felt my sweater move. "What are you doing?" Again, I sounded breathless instead of mad. Nothing was coming out the way I meant it to.

"Pulling up your sweater," Dex said, as if this was obvious. Indeed, he moved it up to my waist. Then his fingertips moved to the waist of my leggings.

"Dex," I said.

"You forgot the other rule," he said as his hands slipped under the elastic. I sucked in a breath at the feel of those hands on me— big, hard, competent hands. My skin zinged and sizzled like a sparkler. "I haven't jerked off. What about you, Parker? Have you gotten off, or are you nice and pent up?"

"I'm fine," I said faintly. I wasn't fine. I was turned on and hot and wet, and Dex was *touching me*. His palms smoothed over my hips, sliding my leggings down. His fingers dipped under the waist of my panties and pulled them down, too.

"You're not fine," Dex said. His voice was low in my ear as he leaned into me, his breath warm on the side of my neck as his hands moved. "You're overworked and stressed out and sad. Who takes care of you, Parker? Who takes the time to make you crazy? When was the last time you lay back and let a man make you come?"

He wasn't saying this. I was having a fantasy, right here in my office—a very real one. I closed my eyes and shook my head because I couldn't think of an answer to his questions. I tried to think of the last time I'd had sex, or even the last time I'd gotten myself off. I couldn't come up with a single memory. It was like my brain had hit a reset button the second he'd put his hands on me.

"You live like a nun," he continued in my ear, his hand moving down under my panties, over my skin. "You're young and hot and so fucking gorgeous, and there's no guy fucking you properly. Every time I look at you I think it's a goddamn crime."

I opened my mouth, finally finding words. "Dex, I—" And then I stopped, because his finger slipped between my legs, over my clit. He dipped into my wetness and pressed his fingertip into me, just at my entrance as I gasped for air.

"Relax," Dex murmured to me. "Call it practice. Call it a warmup. Just give me five minutes and I'll make you come."

We were in my office. *My office.* Outside the closed door the phone was ringing and people were talking, and I didn't care. Because Dex pulled my leggings and my panties down over my hips, and then he lowered himself to his knees on the floor. He pulled my thighs as far apart as they would go. And then he leaned in and put his mouth on me.

It was so good I almost wept.

I leaned back against the desk and let him do it. I let him put his tongue where he wanted—circling my clit, rubbing over my folds, moving inside of me. My body lit up like fire, blood rushing in my ears, the breath rushing in my lungs. His big hands were on the insides of my thighs, and I pressed my legs as far apart as I could, pushing my hips up to give him better access.

Had I thought I had no sex drive? Dex had just poured gasoline on it and lit a match.

He was relentless, torturing me, and in no time I had to grip the desk for support as my eyes drifted closed. I put a hand in his hair—it was soft, the silky strands tangling over my fingers. I forgot about everything, every thought in my head, everything about my life—the only thing that existed was his amazing tongue.

And just like he promised, I came.

It was harsh, almost painful, my muscles clenching as my body moved. How long was it since I'd come? I had no idea. I only knew that I was biting my lip and trying not to scream as I pushed myself hard against his mouth. He met me blow for blow, pulling every last drop of pleasure out of me as if it was the best thing he'd ever tasted. And then, when I was finally wrung out, he let me go.

I gasped for breath as he righted my clothes, then stood. His eyes were darker than I'd ever seen them as he looked at me.

"I hate rules, Parker," he said. "See you in two days."

And then he was gone.

IT TOOK until nine o'clock that night for my phone to ring. It was a lot longer than I'd thought it would take, in fact. Emily must have been busy.

I had just gotten out of a long, luxurious bath. I couldn't remember the last time I'd done that, but tonight it seemed appropriate. I was restless after the encounter with Dex that afternoon, my body pleasantly out of sorts. I had sore muscles from the fierceness of the orgasm I'd had. I could still feel Dex's mouth on me, and I couldn't concentrate. So I poured a glass of hot tea and soaked it all away.

I was wrapped in a thick robe, poking through my fridge for a snack when Emily called. "Evening, Em," I said cheerfully when I answered, even though I already knew why she was calling.

"Why did Dex Riggs come to see you in the salon this afternoon?" she said, wasting no time.

I poked at a bag of baby carrots. I was supposed to be eating a lot of vitamins for fertility. "Who told you?" It was one of the girls at the salon, I knew. It could have been any one of them. They had all seen what happened, they all loved to gossip, and they all had Emily's number.

"Does it matter?" Em said.

"I'm betting Georgie."

"Lauren." She sounded like she was about to burst. This was what we all meant growing up when we said Emily was a drama queen. "Dex Riggs came to the salon and *went into your office with you*. Alone. With the door closed. For almost half an hour."

"Was it that long?" Jesus, Dex was a superstar. It took me a while to get off, though with a concentrated effort I could usually get there. He'd done it in minutes.

"Ryan told Kate that you called the shop looking for Dex on Christmas Eve. You told me you were busy. And now this. I can't think of any reason Dex would be at The Big Do, looking for you. So what's going on?"

"Why can't he come talk to me?" I asked as I pulled the

carrots out of the fridge. I walked to the bathroom and picked up the various jars of fertility supplements I was taking. "Why can't he and I be friends?"

"Honestly?" Em said. "Dex doesn't have any friends. I mean, he knows people. But this is Dex. He doesn't actually have friends."

I stopped with my hand hovering over the kitchen counter, about to put down a jar. Because the unspoken words were right there, hovering in the air: *Neither do you, Lauren. You don't have any friends.*

It was so true it took my breath away. I didn't have friends. I had Em, but she was my twin sister; we were stuck with each other. I had the girls at the salon, but they were my employees. I liked Kate and Tara. But the time I'd spent with Kate was helping her with her new business idea, and I'd never spent time with Tara at all. I'd spent years doing nothing but work and socialize—sort of—with my husband. I'd never had a period as a single girl going out to bars or getting into trouble with my girlfriends. That doesn't happen when you marry your high school sweetheart at twenty.

"You know what?" I said to Em. "I've known Dex for more than half my life. So, yes. We're friends. I think everyone is going to have to get used to it."

"You really think so?" Em said. "You think men and women can just be friends? Without sex?"

That already wasn't in the cards, because Dex and I had an agreement and I'd already had his face between my legs. But that still didn't change my mind. "Yes, I do. Just because you never managed it doesn't mean I can't. Now tell me about the honeymoon. Is it nice in Arizona?"

We talked a little more, and after we hung up I ate my carrots and took my supplements. For the first time I allowed myself to feel a zing of anticipation. Of excitement. Of hope.

I was going to sleep with Dex Riggs.

It was going to be amazing.

And when it was over, I might just be pregnant.

I hadn't felt this alive since the night he'd kissed me ten years ago.

NINE

Dex

OF COURSE it had to snow the night I finally got to sleep with Lauren Parker. Not just a little snow, either—a lot of it, starting in the afternoon and getting heavier as the sky grew darker. Ryan and I worked on the Porsche until three, and then he had to leave to get his seven-year-old son from school. I cleaned up for another half an hour and closed the place down, locking it behind me.

I had just parked at the house, which was still empty because Luke and Emily were away, when my phone rang. It was Lauren.

"Hey," I said when I answered.

"Hey," she said. "I closed the salon in this weather. It's supposed to snow all night. Are we still on?"

"Did we have plans? Remind me, Parker."

"Ha ha," she said flatly. "Very funny, Riggs."

"Relax." I unlocked the guest house door and walked inside. "You'll get your baby, just like I promised. Keep your panties on."

"No," she said. "I don't think I will."

Oh, this was definitely fucking happening. Tonight. "Well, keep them on until I get there," I said. "I'm just getting out of the hot tub. I need to put on my tighty whities and get on my bike."

"Dex!" she said, laughing. Jesus, that sound.

"Don't worry. My sperm is in top condition. I've been feeding it protein and making it do jumping jacks. What have you been doing?"

"Taking supplements. Oh, and having an orgasm, because apparently I needed practice."

That made me remember the session in her office. Part of me still couldn't quite believe she had let me do that. But she'd been so wound up, so needy, that I'd taken a gamble. And I won. I could still taste her when I closed my eyes.

"You did need practice," I told her. "But don't worry. We'll keep at it until you get it right."

"Oh," she said, and it was sort of a sigh, which made me silently crazy. "That sounds good. Really good. I'm stocking up on food right now. I'll be home in half an hour."

We hung up and I gathered a few things into a bag to bring with me. It was snowing, and I was going to be at Lauren's for a while. I had work to do.

I'd never experienced something like this before. The women I met were usually desperate, not very bright, and half crazy. Most of them drank like fish and had more than one man in the revolving door of their life. It suited me just fine; I wasn't a romantic who was looking for a long-term relationship. When I dated at all, which was rarely, I liked women who wanted me gone just as much as I wanted to be gone. Women with hard edges, women who had seen a lot of miles—those were the women I knew.

I'd never had a woman like Lauren. Not ever. Not once. The night I'd kissed her was the closest I'd ever come.

And now she was giving me a chance to get her pregnant.

I stopped what I was doing for a second, taking that in. *A baby.* Holy hell.

My phone rang. I looked at the number and my stomach dropped.

I shouldn't answer it. I knew that. I should just let it go to voicemail, and then again when he hit redial. And again.

Instead, I answered it. "Yeah?"

"Listen, asshole," the voice on the other end said. "I know IAD has talked to you. What did you tell them?"

"I told them to fuck off," I said, which was the truth.

"Yeah? Why don't I believe that, you lying sack of shit?" He sounded pissed. He also sounded like something was getting to him. Like something was maybe worrying him. "They don't need to offer you much of anything to make you roll over. Everyone knows you're at rock bottom. In the gutter. And you're never getting out."

"For a guy who needs my help," I said, "you sure aren't very polite about it."

"You know the rules, Riggs," the voice said. "You keep your mouth shut and we don't kill you. The minute you open your mouth, you're on borrowed time. And so are the others."

"I haven't opened my mouth."

"You will," he said. "Tick tock, asshole." He hung up.

I stood there for a long minute. It didn't matter what I did, what I said. Deep down, I knew it. I was a dead man.

You're at rock bottom. In the gutter. And you're never getting out.

I thought of Lauren. So fucking gorgeous, that woman. She was waiting for me.

She'll never be yours. Not ever.

That was fine. That was for the best.

But I could do this one thing. This one good, amazing thing. I could give Lauren what she wanted, and in the process I could get a few hours with her. A few days, maybe.

And then, when it all went to hell, at least I'd have something to remember.

TEN

Lauren

WHEN VIC AND I DIVORCED, we owned a nice little bungalow in suburban Westlake. I didn't want to be in that house anymore. So Vic bought out my half and I bought a condo downtown, in a small low-rise building made for so-called "executives"—from what I could tell, single people who had no kids and worked too much. Like me.

Surprisingly, I liked it. The condo was the right size, and it was close to everything I needed, as well as being only fifteen minutes from The Big Do. But mostly, I liked the place because it was mine. Just mine. The furniture, the bedding, even the dishes and the silverware—all mine. I'd gone straight from living in my parents' house to our married house, and I'd never had a place that was mine before.

So when I got home and put my groceries away, I felt a good mood settle over me. It was excitement and peace at the same time, which I hadn't thought was possible. Dex was coming over, and we were going to make a baby, and we'd be in my place, in my bed. There was nothing here that had anything to do with my marriage to Vic, and I was glad of it. The divorce had been an upheaval that had left me shaken, but the more that time went by, the more I realized it was the right thing.

Just as I was thinking that, my phone rang. It was Vic.

He didn't call me often; we rarely talked anymore unless it was about something to do with the divorce, like the bank accounts or the credit cards. We'd never had any crazy scenes after the breakup—no calls in the middle of the night, neither of us begging the other for a reconciliation. The entire thing had been civilized. I'd always assumed that was a good thing, that Vic and I had parted ways so peacefully. Now I wondered: Why, exactly, had it been so easy?

"Hey, Vic," I said, answering the phone.

"Hey Lauren," he said. His voice was so familiar, and yet I had no reaction. My heart didn't speed up; my body didn't feel warm at the sound of him. I'd spent ten minutes on the phone with Dex Riggs and felt more excitement than I'd felt in six years of marriage.

Why did I have the feeling that was a bad thing?

"What's up?" I asked Vic when he didn't say anything else.

"Not much," he said. "Is everything okay with you?"

"Sure it is. Why?"

"I don't know. I'm just checking in on you. I feel like I never do that."

I stopped what I was doing and narrowed my eyes. Vic and I never had conversations like this. "I'm great," I said. "Is there something I can do for you?"

"No, no," he said. "I'm good. We haven't talked for a while, that's all."

I put my free hand on the counter. "Vic, what is this?"

He paused again. "Look, I have to tell you something. Don't get mad, okay?"

"What is it?"

"I'm seeing someone."

I was silent. Everything went still.

Vic added, "She's moving in. This weekend."

My lips parted, but no words formed. I just stood there.

"Lauren? Are you there?"

"I'm here," I said. "Who is she?" Because I knew everyone Vic knew. And Vic didn't know very many people.

He sighed. "Shannon Cresswell."

My jaw dropped. "*Shannon Cresswell?* Are you kidding me? I tried out for cheerleading with her when we were in eleventh grade." Neither of us made it, I remembered. Shannon had tried again the next year. I hadn't bothered.

"I know, I know," Vic said. "I wanted to be the one to tell you about this before you heard it from someone else."

"You wanted to be the one to tell me that Shannon Cresswell, who we went to high school with, is moving into my house?"

"It isn't your house," he said. "You made that really clear when you left, Lauren. You didn't want this place to be yours anymore."

He was right. Totally right. And yet I still felt insulted, like my space was violated. "How long has this been going on?"

"A few months. We ran into each other a long time after you moved out, and things just started from there. If you think I was cheating on you, you have it all wrong."

I rubbed my forehead. When I thought back on it, I didn't think Vic had cheated on me. He was a man who went to work, came home, and watched sports all evening. He wasn't exactly a playboy. "Fine," I said. "Okay. You've told me. Your work is done."

"Lauren, don't be mad."

"I'm not mad." I wasn't. I didn't know what I was. Surprised, for sure. A bit shaken. I hadn't thought Vic would find someone else. The idea hadn't crossed my mind, as if Vic was sitting in a museum somewhere, roped off from the world. The idea that I was wrong punctured my pride. But I wasn't mad.

Was I supposed to be mad? I didn't even know anymore.

"I'm moving on," Vic said, his tone annoying the crap out of me, as if he was an all-knowing therapist and I needed his help. "I feel happy again. I think you should find a way to be happy, too."

I was happy until you called, I thought. "Yeah, I'll get on that."

"I know you were unhappy about the baby thing. But you know, now that I look back on it, I think it was for the best that we didn't have a baby. Don't you?"

The words stabbed me so hard I couldn't breathe for a second. I couldn't speak.

"Lauren?"

There was a knock on my door. I'd given Dex the code to get into my building.

"I have to go, Vic," I said. "Goodbye."

I hung up before he could say anything else. I'd hurt so many times while I tried to conceive, in so many ways, that I thought there were no new ways to hurt me. I was wrong.

I put the phone down and unlocked the door, pulling it open. Dex stood there in his jeans and black pea coat. There was snow in his hair.

For a second all I could do was look at him. Those dark blue eyes, his tousled hair, the gorgeous line of his mouth. The easy way he stood, so sure in his own body. The dip of skin at his throat. Everything about him made me feel better. Everything. Even though I'd invited him, I still couldn't believe he was standing here, arrived at exactly the right time.

He lifted one hand and touched my chin. "Are you all right, Parker?"

The brush of his fingertip on my skin brought me back into myself. I grabbed his hand and pulled him inside, closing the door behind him.

ELEVEN

Lauren

"YOU KNOW WHAT?" I said. "I've decided you were right. We should have practiced on Christmas Eve, and every day since. We've been wasting time."

I pulled him into the kitchen, which was dim. I hadn't turned the lights on yet as the snow set in and the sun disappeared. I heard the thump of a bag dropping as Dex followed me.

"Do you want something to eat?" I asked him. "I hope not, because I think we—"

He tugged my hand, pulling me back. He spun me easily so I was facing him. "What's this about?" he asked me.

"Nothing." I tugged at the buttons of his coat and undid them.

"Something's fucked you up."

"Nothing's fucked me up. The opposite, actually." I tried to push his coat off his shoulders, but he put his hands on mine, stopping me. I looked at the buttons of the dark plaid shirt he had on under his open coat, his flat stomach, his hands over mine. We both went still in the hush and the half light of the snow coming down outside the window.

"Lauren," he said, his voice soft. I'd never heard it sound like that before.

"I've been in a fog for months," I said, the words coming out hard. I kept my gaze on his lapels, his chest, his masculine hands. "For years, actually. I've been doing things because I think I'm supposed to. I've been putting one foot in front of the other, and that's all." My hands tightened on his lapels, and his hands tightened over mine. One of his fingers was crooked, as if it had been broken. "I have no joy, Dex," I said. "None. I go from hurting to being numb, then back to hurting again. And whenever I look at you, I remember what I want. What I *want*. It's always so clear when I'm around you."

I raised my eyes to his and found him looking at me, his expression still and intent.

I took a breath. "I want a baby," I told him.

He smiled a little, the corners of his eyes crinkling. "We covered that," he said.

"With you."

His eyebrows went up.

"Not with just anyone," I reiterated. "With you."

I couldn't read his expression then. He swallowed, and I watched his throat work. Then he removed his hands from mine and shrugged his coat off.

He backed me slowly against the kitchen counter. I put my hands on his shoulders, let my palms trail over the line of them. I liked his shoulders. They were hard and strong, shoulders that could carry heavy burdens. Shoulders to grip and to lean on. He pressed closer and I could feel him, smell him. He was familiar to me, and yet he wasn't. I knew what he felt like, but I didn't. I wanted to.

It was so quiet, the world hushed with the snow outside. The light in here was dim and soft, filtered through the snow outside the window. There were no voices or cars outside. It felt like the world had stopped.

Dex leaned in and brushed his mouth over mine, feather-light. I felt that touch through my whole body, from my nipples down between my legs. Every time this man touched me, my body went crazy.

And then I remembered something. "The day you visited me in my office," I said, "you didn't kiss me."

His answer was immediate. "Yes I did."

I tried not to shiver, remembering his mouth on me. He was right. He definitely had kissed me. "On the mouth," I corrected him.

"Is that what you want?" he asked me.

Was he kidding me? My entire marriage was forgotten. I hadn't wanted anything else since I was sixteen. "Yes," I said.

He leaned in. He started slower than he had at the party ten years ago, but it was still a Dex kiss—deep, without apology. I wasn't that girl who had never been kissed anymore, but he was still better than me. He opened my mouth and I let him taste me while I tangled my hands in his hair. But this time I had the presence of mind to move my body up against his, my breasts against his chest through my sweater, my hips against his until he moaned softly in my mouth.

"Fucking hell, Lauren," he said, his voice helpless.

"Keep going," I said.

He took the hem of my sweater and pulled it off over my head. I was wearing a bra and a satin camisole underneath. He undid the buttons of my jeans as I worked the buttons of his shirt. His hands touched the skin of my lower belly and I shivered. I interrupted him to pull off first his button-down, then his tee over his head.

Now I had him shirtless. I'd seen this before on the day of the wedding, but now I got to touch him. I ran my hands over the firm, smooth skin of his biceps, his chest, his stomach. He had dark swirls of hair in a line down his stomach, and I ran my fingertips through it. I felt his muscles clench, like he was keeping control.

"In the bed, Parker," he said.

I agreed. I didn't want to be in the kitchen anymore. I took his hand and led him to my bedroom. I'd made it up nicely this morning, because I knew today was the day. Now we were about to mess it up.

He tossed me on the bed. "Clothes off." It was a command, but I liked it. I took off my boots and my jeans while Dex did the same. I was about to take off my camisole when he got on the bed again, pinning me. He was faster than I was; he was completely naked.

I couldn't see much because he had me pinned on my back, but I could feel him. Big and hard and warm, his body pressed to mine, his cock insistent against the thin fabric of my panties. I'd seen most of him the day of the wedding. Now I wanted to see more.

But that wasn't his plan, at least not yet. Instead he pinned one of my arms to the bed, and with his free hand he dragged down the fabric of my camisole and my bra and sucked my nipple into his mouth.

I gasped, my body moving of its own accord, bucking up into him. My legs fell open and I pushed up onto his cock. He grunted but didn't let up, his tongue moving over my nipple. He let go of my wrist and moved to the other side, pulling the straps off my shoulders and jerking the cloth down to get at me. He scraped his teeth over my nipple and I cried out, my hands gripping his shoulders. I felt his muscles flex beneath my palms.

He moved to my first nipple again. It was torture, because I wanted more. I was hot and throbbing between my legs, my panties wet. I could feel the shape of his cock as he pressed against me, and I wanted it. I ached for it. But he wasn't giving it to me, not yet.

He let my nipple go. "For God's sake, Dex," I said, my voice breathy.

"Roll over," he said. He put a hand on my hip and rolled me onto my stomach. My camisole and bra were twisted up, and he slid a hand up my back, under the camisole, his fingers deftly finding the clasp of the bra. He flicked it open with practiced expertise, then helped me push all of it off over my head. Now I was naked except for my panties, lying on my stomach, Dex braced over me on his knees.

I couldn't see him at all now, only feel him. His hand moved over my back again, a sure stroke from the back of my neck down to my waist, making me shiver. Everywhere he touched me set off fireworks under my skin. I hadn't known it was possible to be touched like this. I was so hot I could barely think.

His hand moved to my hip and he tapped it. "Hips up, Parker." Another command. Apparently I liked taking orders from him, because I eagerly lifted my hips off the mattress. He pulled my panties down, letting them fall to the backs of my knees. Then his hand moved up and cupped the cheek of my ass, his fingertips moving expertly down until they pushed my pussy.

I closed my eyes and gripped the pillow. "Oh my God." He pressed two fingers into me, slow and sure, rubbing me, stretching me. The pleasure spiraled up through me. "Oh my God," I moaned again.

"It's okay if you're loud," Dex said. "You're getting fucked properly for once." He leaned forward over me, his chest to my back, braced on one hand while his other stayed where it was, his fingers moving perfectly inside me. "You should have been more patient ten years ago," he said in a low voice in my ear as I squirmed on his fingers. "I would have done this for you then and saved you a lot of time. We would have been magic. It doesn't matter, though. We'll just have to be magic now." He pulled his fingers out of me and his hand gripped my hip, moving me, positioning me just right. Then I felt the head of his cock against my entrance and he pushed inside me.

I gasped into the pillow. I was wet and slick, and when he pushed into me I could feel myself tightening around him, squeezing him. He made a low, turned-on growl and let go of my hip to brace himself on the bed, pushing into me harder. My panties were still around my knees, but I opened my legs as far as I could, trying to take him deeper.

He sunk all the way in and I felt his forehead drop against the back of my neck. He felt so good that when he paused I practically begged him. "Don't stop."

"Relax," he said, but he moved again, out and in. I knew I was tight; the friction was delicious. Dex was everywhere, inside me, his arms flexing against me, his chest brushing my back, his hips pushing into me. I pushed my hips back against him, meeting him on his next thrust, and I heard him groan.

My body was aching, throbbing. It was so much, and yet it wasn't enough. "I can't," I panted after a minute, "Dex, like this I can't—"

He pulled out of me and flipped me onto my back. Now I could see him, all of him, and he was spectacular. But he still didn't let me look for long. He kissed down my stomach and opened my thighs. "Now you can," he said, and put his mouth between my legs.

My body arched up into him and I grabbed his hair, just like I had in my office. He kissed me like he did then, only this time he was in familiar territory so he knew exactly what to do. My mind went blank as my body lit on fire.

I came long and hard, the orgasm pulsing through me. I could barely catch my breath. Every part of me was oversensitized, and when Dex kissed his way up my body again, I could feel everything. I could feel the tickle of his chest hair against my breasts, the slide of his skin against mine.

He kissed my neck, the lobe of my ear. "I could do that all fucking day," he said. He pushed my knees up to his shoulders and thrust inside me again.

I moaned against him, wild now. I was completely open to him and he fucked me with hard, perfect strokes, taking his own pleasure, his body moving with sharp grace. I dug my nails into his back and held on, loving it, loving how he pushed me and worshiped me, loving how he made me feel. Loving the power I had over him, and the power he had over me.

He stilled and I felt him come, and even though I'd been married it was the most intimate thing I'd ever felt in my life.

We lay there for a moment, both of us out of breath. Then he pushed himself up and looked down at me. His eyes were dark, his hair mussed. He took me in—my sex-tangled hair, my flushed skin, my no doubt sex-drunk expression.

A slow smile touched the corners of his mouth.

"Round one," he said.

TWELVE

Dex

"I THINK I should warn you about something," I said when we were lying in her bed, recovering. Lauren was naked next to me, curled on her side with her hand on my shoulder as I lay on my back. I wasn't used to this. I wasn't a cuddler, and neither was any woman I'd ever been with. In fact, hanging around at all after sex wasn't something I'd ever done. In my world, you always fucked and left.

"What?" she asked. Her voice was a little drowsy, though not outright sleepy. Definitely satisfied. I smiled a little to myself in the dark.

"You're literally the only person who thinks I'm father material," I said. "You know that, right?"

She shifted a little and I felt her chin press against my shoulder. "Is that what you want? To be father material?"

"I don't even know what that is," I said. "My father, remember?"

"Oh. Right."

"Still, if we're going to have a kid, what's your plan?"

She shifted again. I caught a whiff of the smell of her—her skin, her shampoo, and sex. Her bed smelled like her, too, which was fine with me. "Well, when I went to the clinic, I was planning to raise the baby myself. But if you want to be a father, that's even better."

That sent a surprising sting of pain through me. *If you want to be a father, that's even better.* "You think so?"

"Of course," she said as if it was obvious. "Every child needs a father." She paused. "Dex, look at me."

I turned my head. She was propped up on one of her elbows, looking at me. Her hair was long and messy in the best way, her makeup gone. She was fucking gorgeous.

"We can work it out," she said. "If you want to be involved. We can have an agreement so we're both parents."

Was that what I wanted? A few weeks ago I'd been standing by the altar at Luke's wedding, feeling like a stranger on an alien planet. I couldn't see Lauren and I doing the wedding thing with the white picket fence. At least, not yet. She was newly divorced and I was living in the guest house. I didn't even have a home, for fuck's sake. And I didn't even know if she was totally over Vic Voorhees.

But whatever happened between us, if we had a kid...

"Yeah," I said. "I want to be involved."

She smiled, as if that was good news. "Okay, then. If I get pregnant, we'll get a lawyer to draw up something official."

"*When* you get pregnant. And I'm not big on lawyers."

"Tough," she said. "A baby means we have to be real grownups, so we'll do an agreement. Custody, visitation, decision-making. That sort of thing."

"Fine. What about names?"

She shook her head. "No naming the baby. Not until it really happens and I'm in at least the second trimester. I've been through this too many times."

I watched her face. The words she said were painful, but she didn't seem as hurt as she'd been at the wedding. "Okay, I get that. But I might think about names while I'm soaking in my hot tub."

She smiled, which was what I was going for. "You're not big on rules, are you?"

"No. You're learning. While we're talking about lawyers, I have another question. Is Voorhees still in the picture?"

Her jaw dropped open. "What? No. We're divorced."

I shook my head. "Lauren, you're hot. VapoRub is not. He's going to figure out what a mistake he's made and beg for you back. I'll bet money on it."

"Then you're going to lose your money, because he's dating someone."

"Already?" I said. "Who the fuck is dumb enough to date that guy?"

"You want to know who? Shannon Creswell, that's who."

I had to think about the name, which was vaguely familiar. "Dark hair, skinny, captain of the debate team?"

"That's her. Apparently she's debated her way into my house, because she's moving in."

I just looked at her, watching her fume as it sunk in.

"What?" she asked me.

"Your house. You just said she's moving into your house."

"My old house, I mean."

It was too raw, too new. I could tell. "When did you hear about this?"

Her beautiful eyes were dark with annoyance. "Vic called me and told me about it, if you can believe it. He said it was because he didn't want me to hear it from anywhere else, but I'll bet it was just to stroke his ego. Because he's dating someone and I'm not."

"Right," I said. "And let me guess. This happened right before I showed up tonight?"

She looked surprised, then a little guilty. I thought about the way she'd looked when she answered the door, the hurt on her face. The way she'd pulled me into the apartment and practically jumped me. It all made sense. We may have an agreement, but there was no way she was that eager. Not for me.

"Dex," she said.

"I should go." I pushed the sheet off me and sat up, swinging my legs over the side of the bed.

"It isn't what you think," Lauren said behind me.

I pulled on my boxers and stood up. "Is there a shovel somewhere I can use? I probably have to shovel out my car." What time was it? Late. Midnight, maybe. I searched the floor and found my jeans.

"Wait." Lauren pushed the sheet down and got out of bed. I kept my eyes trained to the floor, picking up my clothes. I turned my back, because I couldn't see her naked right now. I heard her closet door open as she looked for something inside.

I put on my jeans, picked up the rest of my clothes, and left the bedroom. I dropped my clothes on a chair in the living room and looked around for my jacket, my keys. The bag I'd brought with me was still on the floor where I'd dropped it when she jumped me. *Jesus, Riggs, you're an idiot. You always have been.*

I pulled on my tee as she came out of the bedroom behind me. "Dex, wait," she said again. "I didn't mean it like that. I'm sorry."

"It's fine," I said, sitting down to put on my boots. I could still see snow coming down out the window. Fuck, it was going to take me ages to get out of here. It had been fine before, when I'd assumed I'd spend the night.

Lauren stepped in front of me. She had put on a robe—a thin, knee-length thing that barely covered her. Even as she pulled it tight and belted the waist, I could see every line and curve of her body. I dropped my gaze to my boots again.

"I think you're taking this wrong," she said.

"I'm taking it exactly right. We had an arrangement, that's all. Nothing else. We aren't dating, like you say. We're just getting this thing done." I looked up at her. "We can fulfill the agreement. But I'd appreciate it if you'd be honest and tell me straight if you're using me because you're pissed at something your ex did."

"Dex, no." She ran her hands through her sex-messy hair, distress on her face. "Damn it, I've screwed this up."

"I told you, you haven't. We have a few more days. I'll stick to the agreement."

"I don't care about the agreement!" she cried. "I care that you're shutting down on me."

She was right about that. I was. I could feel it happening, the doors closing, the windows shutting. I was becoming the guy who didn't give a shit, because the guy who didn't give a shit was the one who had got me through life so far. When your mother left you like a piece of garbage and your father didn't treat you any better, the guy who doesn't give a shit is the only guy you have.

What was I thinking, considering raising a kid? I was the last person who should raise a kid. What a stupid idea that was.

I stood up, but Lauren didn't move from her place in front of me. She stayed close, so close I could feel the brush of her robe and smell her. I'd have the smell of her on me for days. I already knew I'd torture myself with it.

She put her hands on my shoulders, looked into my eyes. "Dex, don't go," she said.

I looked at her and I felt a bolt of panic. There was no other word for it. I remembered how she'd felt beneath me, her nails digging into me, the way she'd let go. We'd been incredible together, just like I knew we'd be.

It had never been like that with anyone before. *I'd* never been like that before.

Which meant she could wreck me.

I locked it down. I made myself sound cold, in control. Like the guy who doesn't give a shit. "We need to be clear, Parker," I said. "If you want to use me, I'll consider it. But you have to be honest."

A muscle twitched in her jaw as she fought not to flinch. "I'm not using you," she said. She kept her hands on my shoulders, her palms warm there. "I promise you I'm not."

"Yeah? What would you call it, then?"

"Me having a moment of stupidity. And I don't mean the part where we had sex. I mean the part where I let what Vic does get to me." She sighed, and her chest moved under the sheer robe, which I tried not to look at. "I can be petty, okay? Maybe you should know that about me. I can be very, very petty."

I hesitated, amused despite myself. "That's your big flaw, Parker? You're petty?"

"I try not to be," she said seriously. "I try to be the bigger person. But I don't always manage it. And do you want to know the truth? I don't even care that Vic is dating Shannon. It's the house that got to me. I *picked* that house. Vic didn't even want it. He wanted us to live with his parents."

I couldn't help it; I laughed. "You're shitting me."

"No. I know, right? I put my foot down and we bought the house instead. Now he gets to pretend like it was all his idea." She sighed, as if she realized how that sounded. "I'm not going to lie, Dex. I may have some shit to unpack from this divorce."

"Yeah, well, unpack it," I said. "We're not getting married, so take your time. Everyone has crap that they carry around."

She put her hands on my shoulders again. Like she couldn't

quite resist touching me. I tried not to feel the jolt of warmth it sent down into me. "Okay, we're not getting married," she said. "We've established that. But I guess I should have asked. Are we dating?"

I narrowed my eyes at her. "That seems kind of official. I'm not bringing you wine and roses, Parker."

Instead of being offended, she smiled. "Oh, good. I've been the wine and roses route. I like your way better." She stepped closer, putting her arms lightly around my neck and pressing against me. "Please stay."

I had to push my gaze away from her, past her to the window. She was sexy, she was mostly naked, and it was snowing like hell outside. We were electric in bed. And she wanted me to stay.

Most of all, she was Lauren fucking Parker.

I already knew I wasn't going to say no.

Still, I kept my expression stony as I turned back to her. "Okay. Two things. First of all, that was a free pass. If you get one, then so do I. I get a free pass when I fuck up, because I inevitably will."

"You get a free pass," she said, her body all warm and nice-smelling against mine. "Agreed. What's the other thing?"

"Take the robe off and get on the kitchen counter."

THIRTEEN

Dex

THERE WAS a split second when I thought it wouldn't happen, but my instincts knew better. Lauren breathed in, her chest moving against mine. Her eyes widened.

Then she dropped her arms from around my neck, stood back, and put a hand to the knot of her robe.

I was learning this about her. She wouldn't admit it, but she liked to be told what to do. It turned her on. I figured it probably came from having to be the boss all the time. It made her hot when she wasn't the boss for once.

Fine with me. I liked being the one in charge.

Still, we'd just had a fight, and she couldn't quite give it up. "You first," she said. "Take your shirt off."

Did she want me to do it, or did she want me to argue? I went with my instincts again. I reached to the back of my neck, pulled my tee off, and dropped it. "That's all you get," I said. "Get naked. Now."

Lauren smiled at me. She untied her robe and dropped it to the floor.

Damn, she was gorgeous naked. I'd seen it only an hour ago, but it didn't matter. I didn't think I'd ever get enough. Those perfect breasts, the curve of her hips, her lean legs. Her honey-colored hair tumbling down her back. I had to remember not to stand there dumbfounded like an idiot. Instead I moved toward her as she backed up to the island between the kitchen and the living room. When she got there I put my hands on her hips and lifted her onto the edge so she was right where I wanted her.

I leaned in and kissed her neck, her collarbone, down to her breasts. She took a shuddering breath as I ran my tongue over her nipples, her body tensing. She lifted a hand from the countertop and ran it over the back of my neck.

It was too much, that touch. "Hands down, Parker," I said. "You're going to need to hold on."

She obeyed, putting her hand on the counter to brace herself as I kissed down, down. "Oh," she said in that soft, delighted way she had when she realized where I was going. "You... You really like to do this."

"You have no idea," I said, going lower, opening her thighs. There was nothing I liked better than the smell of her, the taste of her. I wasn't lying when I said I could do this all night. Lauren's pussy was the best thing I'd ever seen in my entire life.

She leaned back on her arms, giving me access, and I kissed her. Long and deep, the way she liked it. I went slow and thorough, tasting her, savoring her. In the times I'd done this already, I'd found the spots that were her favorites. I'd found exactly what made her go fast and what made her go slow. The only thing to do now was get better with practice, so I used everything I'd learned.

I've always been a good learner when I truly apply myself. This was no different. In a few minutes Lauren was melted on the countertop, on the edge of coming, making sounds that were burned into my brain. When she got close enough I pulled back and bit the tender flesh on the inside of her thigh, making her flinch and gasp. Then I kissed my way up her stomach again.

"Dex," she moaned in disappointment.

"Patience," I said, lowering a hand to undo my jeans. I was hard as a fucking anvil. I pushed them down my hips, torturing myself with the drag of my cock along her skin. I didn't touch her where she wanted, leaving her aching and ready.

When I kissed my way back up over her breasts she managed to make a full sentence at last. "We couldn't do this on the bed?"

I licked her collarbone. "Have you ever been fucked on a kitchen counter?"

"No."

"Then I'm fucking you right here." I dragged my teeth along the skin of her neck. "Be a little adventurous, Lauren."

She shivered, then leaned up and kissed me, her mouth soft and hot. I kissed her back, working her up a little again, then broke it off. She sighed against my mouth. "You are so good at that," she said.

No compliments. Like her touch earlier, they were too much. "Stroke me," I told her, my voice rough.

She reached down between us and took my cock in her hand, stroking it up and then down again. I realized my mistake, because I nearly came right then. Jesus, my cock was happy whenever Lauren was anywhere near it. "Harder," I told her, because if she did what she was doing, I wouldn't last.

She bit her lip and squeezed me a little, watching my reaction. There was pain, just enough to make my orgasm retreat. I felt my body tense, my jaw flex. "Again," I said, the word harsh.

She squeezed me again, stroking up to the tip. Another jolt of pain that sent my orgasm back, though it was still there, waiting. A sound escaped my throat and her eyes widened a little as she watched me.

"Jesus, Dex," she said. "That's the hottest thing I've ever seen."

I dropped my forehead to her shoulder and took her wrist, moving her hand off me and onto herself. "Touch yourself," I ordered her. "Make yourself come."

I was done waiting. When she put her fingertips to her pussy I positioned myself and thrust into her, pressing her into the counter. She made a sound of pleasure that sent electricity straight down my spine. I pulled out and thrust into her again, harder this time, feeling it through my cock, my whole body.

Then, as she stroked herself, I did it again. And again.

Lauren's head dropped back, her hair brushing the counter. Her breasts shook as I fucked her. And she kept her hand where it was as she built up and up. I felt every second, every pulse under her skin. I heard every breath, every sound. And then, with a cry, she came, squeezing me from root to tip.

I let go and came, braced over her on the counter, breathless, my muscles locked tight. I gave her everything. I tried not to, but I fucking failed.

This woman was going to wreck me.

It was only a matter of time.

FOURTEEN

Lauren

WE REOPENED The Big Do on the second of January. The first week after New Year's was always quiet, because everyone had gotten their hair done—and blown their budget—in December. There was a customer out front getting highlights while the other girls sipped coffee and gossiped. I was in the back office as usual, looking at December's reconciliation reports.

The door opened and Emily walked in. She wore slim-cut jeans, knee-high boots, and a black zip-up coat. Her blonde hair was tousled from the winter wind. "Hey, sis!" she said brightly.

Of course she was cheerful. She'd just gone on a honeymoon. I searched for the tiny voice in my head that was bitter, and I couldn't find it. I only felt happy to see her. Maybe my bitterness had been orgasmed out of me.

"You're back," I said. I stayed in my chair and I didn't hug her. Em and I were fraternal twins, but we weren't very demonstrative. We didn't do the huggy-kissy thing.

"I am," she said, dropping dramatically into the chair opposite the desk, as if exhausted. "What a fantastic trip."

"I bet Arizona was a lot warmer than here."

"I suppose. We weren't there very long. We had to make the drive back."

I narrowed my eyes at her. "You drove all the way to Arizona, just to turn around and come back again?"

She shrugged. "Arizona wasn't the point, really. The point was the road trip." She smiled. "And the road trip was amazing. I have to talk to Tara and Kate ASAP. Being married to a Riggs brother is *awesome*."

I politely looked at my computer screen, not mentioning the fact that I'd been screaming the last single Riggs brother's name for the past three days. "I'm glad you had fun."

"So what did I miss?"

"Um." I looked at some of the papers on the desk. "We had a pre-New Year's Eve rush, as usual. One of the washing sinks is a little clogged. Melanie the nail tech needs two weeks off to get married, and I'm looking for someone to replace her."

"No, Lauren. What did I miss with you?" Emily leaned forward. "You do have a life outside this place, right?"

"Yes, I do." I tucked a lock of hair behind my ear and told my sister a bald-faced lie. "Not much happened with me."

"What did you do for New Year's?"

"Stayed home." This was true. Dex was at my place on New Year's Eve. We'd had incredible, incredible sex. I wondered where we were exactly at midnight. In the shower, maybe. There was definitely shower sex, another thing on the list of things I'd never done before. Six years of marriage and I'd never done shower sex. I hadn't thought it was even possible. It turned out that with Dex Riggs it was not only possible, it was also hot and wild and amazing.

I had sore muscles. *Sore muscles.* How the hell did that happen?

"That's it?" Emily said. "You just sat home in your pajamas? You're single now. I thought maybe you'd go out and get drunk at a bar somewhere."

I leaned back in my chair and looked at her. "Really? Have you literally ever met me, Em?"

"You need to live it up, sis," Em said. "Get out there. Take some risks. Just because you're divorced doesn't mean you need to sit home for the rest of your life." She motioned to me, her hands going up and down. "You're hot, after all."

You're hot, Dex had said. I hadn't wanted to admit how much I liked it when he said that. It seemed so shallow. Still, right now I felt like someone who was hot. So I smiled at my sister. "I know."

"Ha. That's better." Em smiled back at me. "By the way, I was just at Riggs Auto Two and saw your *friend* Dex."

"That's nice." *How is he? Did he look good? Did he mention me?*

"They're working on that expensive Porsche. Luke couldn't stand not seeing it in person. He went straight to Riggs Auto Two when we got back." She rolled her eyes. "I think if he wasn't already married, he'd find a way to marry that car."

"They all would," I said. Dex had told me about the Porsche. He'd lit up when he described it, but there was wariness in his eyes too, as if he thought it was too good to be true. "The Riggs boys all love their cars."

"I know." Em closed her eyes and inhaled, waving her hands toward her face. "It's so nice to be back here with all this estrogen. I'm taking it in."

I laughed and shook my head. My sister might be a little crazy, but she was one of a kind. I couldn't remember what it was like the eight years she was away. That entire time—the time I'd been with Vic—felt like a long hibernation, tucked away from real life. I pushed my chair back and stood. "Well, inhale all you want. This is your gig again. I'm going to go work on my other career."

"Seriously, thanks for filling in. I owe you one. Oh, and I guess I'll see you tomorrow night."

"Tomorrow night?" I said, stepping around the desk and grabbing my coat.

"It's Jace's birthday," Em said. "The guys are all going out for a beer and a few games of pool. The girls are going, too."

I stared at her. "The Riggs brothers are hanging out socially? Together? On their own time? By choice?"

"I know. It's weird, right? But Ryan suggested it, and Jace said he would go, and Luke thought it was a good idea. Dex was harder to convince, but he eventually said yes. I mean, I thought they'd never hang out again after the disaster that was the bachelor party."

Everyone knew about the bachelor party, which had landed Dex and Ryan briefly at the Westlake police station for public fighting. "Okay," I said. "I might come by, but I leave if there's violence."

Emily laughed as I zipped up my coat. "Come for the beer, stay for the violence," she said. "The Riggs brothers know how to have a good time."

I WAS UNLOCKING my car when my phone rang. I pulled it out of my pocket. It was Dex.

"What's up?" I said when I answered.

"Folic acid," Dex said.

"What?"

"Folic acid. It says you need that if you're getting pregnant. Are you taking that?"

"Um, yes," I said, opening the driver's door and getting in. "I've been taking it for a long time. What's this about?"

"What about zinc?" he said. "It says here you need zinc. Are you eating zinc?"

I felt myself smiling. "Dex."

"What the hell is Coenzyme Q10? Are you taking that too?"

"Dex," I said again as I closed the door. "Did you just Google fertility vitamins?"

"I had no idea this was so complicated," he replied. "I'm in the back office of the shop with the door closed. Ryan thinks I'm fucking nuts. I just looked up one thing, and now I've been reading for half an hour. This is insane."

"It isn't complicated for everyone," I said. "Remember Mindy Green in high school? She has two kids by two different guys already." It was one of those things people talked about when they didn't know you were trying to get pregnant, when they didn't know how it hurt to hear it. I'd probably heard that story a dozen times.

"Yeah, well, not by me," Dex said. "This is my first go-round. How do you feel? Do you feel pregnant?"

I turned on the car, blasted the heater. "Dex, it's been two days. It doesn't work like that."

"It says here you can feel it as early as a week."

"Or not for a month."

He grunted. "Fuck, this is frustrating."

"I know. Welcome to my world for the last two years. It's been fun."

He sighed. "Should I fuck you some more? Would that help?"

I leaned back in my seat. Only Dex Riggs could make me laugh and flush with arousal at the same time. For a minute the whole world fell away and there was just me and him. "Why do I feel like your suggestion is a little self-serving?" I asked.

"I'm just saying, Parker. I'm willing to step up."

"I bet you are," I said, laughing again. Then I remembered the session on the kitchen counter, and I flushed hot all over. Every time I looked at that counter I had a vivid memory. I wasn't sure I'd be able to cook ever again. "You've seen the calendar," I said, trying to be rational. "It isn't on the schedule."

"Screw the schedule," he said. "I have motility happening over here, and you're wasting it."

Okay, he was freaking ridiculous. But we weren't a thing, and this was only a baby project. Besides, I was still sore from New Year's. "I'll see you tomorrow, Dex," I said. "Jace's birthday thing."

"Fine," he said, accepting defeat. "But no alcohol, Parker. I'll be watching." He hung up.

I had no idea how he did it. But I was in a good mood for the rest of the day.

FIFTEEN

Dex

JACE WAS the youngest Riggs brother. He was also the smartest of us, a guy who had stacks of books, even before he had a lot of reading time in prison. After me, he'd taken the second-most amount of shit from our father, because Dad hated smart people almost as much as he hated me. Also, Jace had never had a birthday party. None of us had.

I wasn't even sure we were having one now. I knew that we were at the Guardhouse bar—Luke, Jace, Ryan, and me. I knew that we were shooting pool. And I knew that, as usual, my brothers were getting on my nerves.

"There's definitely something wrong with you," Luke said to me as he chalked his cue. "You don't seem like the same Dex."

"Shut up, dickbag," I said.

Luke nodded. "Okay, that part's the same. But there's something else different."

"It's his hair," Ryan said, picking up his beer from the bar. "He's been washing it. And he got it cut."

"Is that a new shirt?" Jace added, sipping his beer and smirking at me.

"I can't believe I'm related to any of you," I said, racking up the balls on one of the pool tables. "Are we done talking about my hair and my clothes? If you want, I can give you my skin care regime."

"That isn't it," Ryan said, pointing to the glass of water I'd put on the bar table behind me. "You're not drinking. And the joints are gone."

"Ah, that's it," Luke said, relieved. "I'm seeing you clearly instead of through a weed haze. It makes you look entirely different."

Listen: I grew up with these three idiots. And I was the oldest, which meant there was a lot of ribbing for them to get revenge for. The potshots were expected.

I wasn't going to admit they were right. The haircut, the new shirt. The weed and the drinking. "I told you, I have a stomachache," I said to Luke. It was the best explanation I could come up with for not having a beer, when pretty much every particle of my body longed for one. Getting drunk sounded fantastic right about now. But I'd promised Lauren, and I wasn't off the hook yet. Not until we knew she was pregnant.

And if my brothers knew about *that* little scheme—the ribbing would be insane.

"I call bullshit on the stomachache," Ryan said. "I work with him every day, and he's never hung over anymore. If he has a stomachache, he's had it for over a week."

"I have had a stomachache," I said. "It's from listening to you being an idiot all day."

"Maybe he's on a diet," Jace said, picking up his cue and advancing to the table.

"Maybe there's a woman," Luke said, stepping up to take Jace on for the first match.

"I've never cleaned up for a woman in my life," I said. First rule of having three brothers: Always be on the defensive. Never show fear. Even if you're lying.

Jace and Luke flipped a coin, and Jace got the first shot. He leaned over to take the break, aiming his cue like the expert he was. Jace was unbeatable at pool; Luke was going to lose, badly. I was saved from further gossip by the door opening and the women coming in: Emily, Tara, Kate, and—trailing in last—Lauren. She didn't look at me. I sipped my water and turned back to the game.

To be honest, I wasn't sure how we were playing this. We weren't a thing, which was fine. We were friends, maybe. But I'd just spent several nights fucking Lauren, and it was the best thing that had ever happened to me. Oh, and it was possible she was carrying my kid. To say it was complicated was an under-statement.

To make it even more complicated, I wanted to fuck her again. Of course I did. She had those long legs, that perfect ass in her jeans. The cool way she tugged her mittens off and put them in her pockets. Her hair tied back in a loose, messy braid that I wanted to undo. She was still Lauren Parker, the good girl and cop's daughter of Westlake High. Except now I knew what every inch of her looked like naked.

The women went to the bar and ordered their drinks, and I heard Lauren order an iced tea. "Come on," Emily said to her. "Not even one drink?"

"Iced tea," Lauren reiterated calmly. "I can be the designated driver. Besides, I have a headache."

I pretended I hadn't heard. That was too close for comfort. We needed to come up with a better story.

But no one said anything, and we settled in to talking and

pool. Emily programmed songs into the bar's juke box—some modern country and western singer the women all claimed was hot. Emily took over Jace's spot and tried to beat Luke at pool. Ryan talked quietly to Kate for a minute, his arm lightly around her waist as he said something in her ear, making her light up and smile, then laugh. Ryan's son was with a sitter for a few hours, and from what Ryan told me at work, they didn't get a ton of time alone together. My brother was making the most of it, touching her lightly every chance he got, as if he couldn't help himself.

Another round of drinks was ordered. We shot pool. Lauren came over and perched on a bar stool next to where I was standing, watching as Ryan took on Emily, who was determined to win. "You're drinking water, I noticed," she said to me. "I approve."

"Thank you, your majesty," I said, keeping my eyes on the game.

She smiled and sipped her iced tea. I watched her from the corner of my eye. "Admit it. I'm a good influence on you."

"I don't need a good influence, Parker."

"Yes, you do. Are you worried everyone is going to find us out?"

I shrugged. "I thought we were keeping it quiet."

"You could at least look at me."

I turned and looked at her. Her blue-gray eyes met mine and held there, and her cheeks went red. "Oh, okay," she said softly. "You should probably stop."

I turned away to the game again. "Yeah, I know."

Now that she was next to me, I could admit it: I wanted to touch her. I wanted to lean in and get the smell of her, the feel of her hair. I wanted to get out of here and get her alone, do all the things to her I'd done before, but do them even better this time. Instead my phone buzzed silently in my back pocket and I pulled it out, looking at the number as my stomach sank. "I have to take this," I said to her. "I'll be right back."

I walked to the hallway outside the bathrooms and took the call. "What the hell do you want?" I said. "I told you not to call me anymore."

"Dex." It was Kevin Blanchard, a lawyer I knew from Detroit. "Have you been watching the news?"

"No, I haven't been watching the news." I didn't even own a TV.

"Well, you should start paying attention. I'm hearing through the grapevine that the investigation into the Stone-haven operation is heating up. There's a new chief of police and a new mayor, and the pressure is on. It's only a matter of time."

Everything stopped for a minute. My head spun. I felt sick. "What are you talking about?"

"I'm talking about charges, Dexter," Kevin said. He liked to call me Dexter, probably just to fuck with me. He was an asshole like that. "I'm talking about a whole slew of them, of the entire operation getting reopened and dragged into the light. I'm talking about the fact that you need a lawyer."

"I don't need a fucking lawyer," I said, trying to keep it together. "I was there that night when the operation went down. But I didn't do anything wrong."

"Then you're going to have to testify to that fact."

"I am not fucking testifying." I thought about the phone call I'd had, the voice I knew from another life. *The minute you open your mouth, you're on borrowed time, and so are the others. Tick tock.*

"You might not have a choice," Kevin said. "If this thing blows up, it's going to blow up big. And you're going to be in the middle of it."

I put a hand against the wall to steady myself. Because this, right here, was the thing. The thing that had ruined whatever life I might have had.

People looked at Dex Riggs, and they saw a washed-up cop. A failure. A guy who smoked and drank too much, who didn't cut his hair, who didn't buy new shirts. They saw a guy who walked the edge because he wanted to. And I knew what people said: that I was flat-out fucking crazy.

What they didn't see was a guy who was being eaten alive from the inside. Every minute of every day. Like he'd swallowed acid and it was festering in his stomach, pumping through his bloodstream. A guy who had had to make a choice and live with it.

There was a reason I was fucking crazy, but I couldn't tell anyone. Because if I did, I was dead. And so were three innocent people.

Tick tock.

"What do you want?" I said to Kevin. Outside the hallway, I heard laughter and someone raising their voice, like they were making an announcement. "Why do you keep calling me?"

"I want you to hire me," Kevin said. "You need me, Dexter. My retainer starts at four thousand dollars. Then we can talk."

I laughed. I didn't have four thousand dollars. Not even close. "I'm not hiring you, because I don't need a lawyer."

"You do, my friend," Kevin said. "I know it sucks to have me be the one to break it to you, but you very much do. You have to pick sides here, or one side or the other is going to do it for you."

"Not if I refuse."

"You can't fucking refuse." Kevin sounded serious, some of the glee fading from his voice. "That's what I'm trying to tell you. I'm trying to do you a favor. But some people always learn the hard way."

"Then I guess I'm one of those people," I said, and hung up.

I stood there for a minute, trying to collect myself. I was a man on a high wire with nothing but air beneath me. I not only walked there, I lived there. I had been living there for years. Crazy Dex Riggs and his death wish. People had no idea.

Lauren came around the corner, concern on her face. "Hey," she said. "You're missing out over there. People are wondering where you are."

I put my phone in my pocket. *Get a grip, Riggs. Handle it.* "What am I missing?"

"Jace and Tara are engaged." She smiled. "Another wedding, Dex. You were right—I'm glad I still have my dress. I hope you still have your suit."

Fuck. My brothers and I might not be close, but they were trying to build lives. Build families. They were trying to do something with their lives. Ryan had Kate and his kid, Luke was married, and Jace was tying the knot. The business was doing well and we had that Porsche at Riggs Auto Two. Things were going good for my brothers for the first time in their lives—because they'd earned it.

I was only going to drag them down.

I was doing it already.

I looked at Lauren and knew I would drag her down, too.

"I have to go," I said. I brushed past her and walked into the bar, picked up my coat. People were talking, hugging Tara. I caught Jace's eye as I walked for the door.

"Later, asshole," I said to him. I pointed to Tara. "Don't fuck that up."

Jace nodded. "Fuck you, Dex," he said with a straight face. Because my brothers and I never bothered with *hello* or *goodbye* like normal people. And we weren't going to start now.

I couldn't help it—I glanced back over my shoulder. Lauren was standing at the back of the room, a frown on her face as she watched me. I'd disappointed her. I'd disappointed all of them.

They were going to have to get used to it. I already was.

SIXTEEN

Lauren

THERE WAS SOMETHING WRONG. Dex wouldn't just leave like that; something had shaken him up. I'd never seen Dex shaken up before. No one had. Except I'd swear on my life he was shaken up just now.

I was the only one who thought so, unfortunately. Everyone else just shrugged when Dex left. "Does he need a reason?" Ryan asked when I wondered out loud why he had left. "I don't know if you noticed, but Dex is kind of an asshole."

"He left our engagement party, too," Luke pointed out. "He has a bit of a problem with acting like a normal human."

It was true. He had left Luke and Emily's engagement party after Luke had named him best man. He'd walked out without telling anyone, just like he'd done tonight. Anyone looking on would think it was his pattern. He hated these sappy, emotional events. It went with the Dex that everyone knew.

But I'd seen him in the back hallway, putting the phone in his pocket. I'd seen his face, the expression on it before he'd shut it down and become his usual self again.

"Something's wrong," I said.

"He probably got a call from his weed dealer," Luke said. "Emergency pickup."

That was Dex; everyone knew him. He was crazy, he was a mess, he smoked and drank too much. He got in fights, including the recent one with Ryan that got them both hauled into the police station. Dex was hopeless. He'd always been hopeless, and everyone figured he always would be.

And still, I wanted to shout at everyone. I was starting to see how Dex wore the mask that he did—how skillfully he'd fooled everyone into thinking he was something he wasn't. At least, not all the time.

The question was, why?

I tuned back into the conversation when Kate said, "What actually happened when he left the Detroit PD? Does anyone know?"

"Only rumors," Luke said. "There was something about him quitting to avoid corruption charges coming down."

"I heard one about him leaving because he couldn't hack it," Jace said. "Like a nervous breakdown."

I thought about Christmas Eve, about Dex and me in that shitty bar, talking. I'd asked him if he was corrupt. *The answer to that is complicated,* he'd said.

"PTSD is pretty common in cops," Tara said. "I treat them in my counseling office from time to time. It usually starts with sleeplessness, depression, and irritability and goes from there."

Luke shook his head. "Jesus, that's pretty much Dex in a nutshell. Then again, he's been like that most of his life. Long before he was a cop, for sure."

"Drug and alcohol use," Ryan chimed in. "Don't forget that part."

"Dex hasn't had drugs or alcohol for over a week," I said. "He quit them no problem."

Everyone went quiet, looking at me.

"What?" I looked around. "I told you, we're friends."

"How do you know when he quit?" Emily asked me. She had her laser-eyed twin sister gaze on me, missing nothing. She looked pointedly at the iced tea in my hand, then back up to my face.

"Because he told me," I said.

"And why did he quit?"

"You'd have to ask him that."

There was another second of quiet while everyone looked at me. Then Ryan said, "I asked him about it once. About what happened in Detroit, one day while we were working."

"And what did he say?" Kate asked.

Ryan scratched his chin. "He said I should believe all of the rumors, because all of them were true. Then he said I should shut up and get back to work, because my shitty baseball career wasn't going to pay any bills."

Luke and Jace laughed. Kate shook her head.

"He's an asshole, but sometimes he nails it," Luke said. "He's gotten us out of a few jams recently. We should probably be grateful."

"I owe him a lot," Jace agreed. "After what happened with Tara's ex, I probably wouldn't be here but for him. He wouldn't let me thank him, either."

"Where are you going?" Emily asked me.

I was putting my coat on, zipping it up. "Home to bed," I said.

"It isn't even late."

I raised my eyebrows at her. "Yeah, well, some of us haven't just come back from a nice romantic honeymoon. I've been working, and I'm tired."

Her eyes narrowed. "I swear, sis, whatever is going on, I'm going to get it out of you."

"You can try." I gave her a sweet smile, the one that drove her up the wall, and I said the phrase that used to make her crazy when we were kids. "Nighty night, Em."

I walked out of there and I got in my car. But I didn't go home.

Because his brothers could say whatever they wanted, but I knew something was wrong.

I just had to figure out what it was.

I DIDN'T THINK he'd answer the door at first. I stood outside the Riggs guest house and banged my fist on it. "Dex, I know you're in there. Open up." It was a repeat of Luke and Emily's wedding day, except now there was snow on the ground and I wasn't in a bridesmaid's dress.

He finally opened the door. He had taken off the button-down shirt he had on in the bar, and now he was wearing a worn white tee and low-slung jeans, his feet bare. His hair was mussed and the dark blue of his eyes sliced straight through me, making me hurt and want at the same time. He blocked my way through the door with one long, muscled arm braced over the doorway in the cold.

"Lauren, go home," he said.

"No."

"I'm serious. Just go."

"What was that phone call?"

His eyes flickered with some emotion I couldn't name, and then they went cold again. "It was a woman," he said, his voice flat. "She called to see if I wanted to fuck her tonight. I said yes."

It hurt. A slice of pain straight down my breastbone, sharp as a knife. I might be vulnerable, but I wasn't a fool. "I don't believe you. You're lying."

"You think so? Here, let me show you." Dex pulled his phone from his back pocket and swiped it on. He scrolled through his texts, found the one he wanted, and handed the phone to me.

It was from someone named Cindy. *Sexy Dex, call me!* She wrote. *I am free 2night.* The words were followed by a string of heart emojis. The text was timestamped an hour ago.

He hadn't replied. Then again, when I saw him in the bar he was on the phone, so maybe he'd called her instead. The slice of pain again, pure and hard through my chest.

I looked up into his face and saw nothing. A careful mask without a flicker of emotion in it. But when I looked in his eyes, I saw something different.

And it made me furiously angry. I hurled the phone past him into the room, hearing it hit the wall with a bang. "You're full of shit!" I yelled at him. "You're saying this to hurt me, and I don't know why. But I know you. And you are *full of shit.*"

A muscle twitched in his jaw. "You don't know me at all."

"Really?" I put both hands on his chest and pushed him back into the guest house, following him in and slamming the door closed behind me. "You invited her over for a screw, did you? Well, I'll just wait with you." I walked in and sat down on a chair. "I'd like to meet this Cindy. Is she hot?"

"Jesus, Lauren," Dex said. "Get the message, will you? We had our thing. We did our biology experiment. I hope it works out for you, but my part is done. I'm going to smoke some weed, get drunk, fuck someone else, and move on."

I tried not to flinch at the words *biology experiment*, but I didn't succeed. I'd never seen him like this, so angry and so cold.

And yet he'd called me Lauren. Not Parker—Lauren.

It took every ounce of strength I had, but I pushed through the pain and said the words. "You're not going to do any of those things." I motioned around me at the guest house. "There's no liquor here, no weed. And no Cindy. So tell me what that phone call really was."

He leaned over my chair, bracing himself on the arms, looking into my face. His jaw was set, his gaze like granite. "Get this through your head, Parker," he said, as if he was summoning the words through the pain too. We both were. "I'm not a guy you want anything to do with. I never have been. So get out."

It was just like that night ten years ago at his party. *I'm kicking you out, Parker.* "You don't mean it," I said to him.

"Find someone else," he said. "Someone good. Someone who knows how to be a real person. Someone who wasn't fucked up from day one."

I looked into his face and I knew. "This has something to do with Detroit," I said. "Something to do with you and the Detroit PD. This has nothing to do with a woman at all. Are you going to tell me you were a corrupt cop, Dex? Is that the next lie?"

He went still for a long minute, looking at me in silence. His arms were so tense, his body so hard, I thought if I touched him he might shatter.

"Tell me," I said, looking into his eyes, challenging him. "Say the words. *I was a corrupt cop, Lauren.* Look me in the eye and say it."

Still he was silent, wrestling with himself. I could see pain deep in his eyes, in every line of his face.

"Say it," I said again.

He held, and then he closed his eyes and sagged a little, his shoulders going slack. I let out a breath I hadn't realized I was holding.

"Lauren," he said, his voice taut. "You're fucking killing me."

I touched him then. I reached up and stroked a thumb along his cheekbone, cupped his jaw. "Am I?" I asked. "It seems to me that you're killing yourself."

He kept his eyes closed, but he didn't move away. "Have you ever made a decision and wondered if it was the right one?" he asked. "I mean a big decision. One that followed you everywhere you went. One that haunts you when you sleep, because no matter how many times you go over it, you don't know if you chose wrong."

"No," I admitted. "The hardest decision I ever made was to ask for a divorce, and the minute I did it I knew in my gut that I had done the right thing. To be honest, I've almost never looked back."

"That must be nice." Dex opened his eyes and looked at me. "You have a lot of spine, Parker. You always have."

I'd never thought of myself that way, but I liked it. I liked the way Dex saw me. I was always a different woman when I was with him. I was the woman I wanted to be.

I leaned up and kissed him, gently exploring. He always told me how he felt when he kissed me. He resisted for a brief second, and then he kissed me back, both of us going slowly, as if we were both bruised. I opened my mouth and slid my tongue between his lips, tasting him, and he groaned, the sound hot and vulnerable as he dragged his teeth lightly over my lower lip.

I pulled back and unzipped my coat, dropping it. I pulled off my sweater. Still sitting in the chair, with Dex looking down at me, I unclasped my bra and dropped it too.

"Jesus, Lauren," he said.

I pushed up the hem of his T-shirt, and he pulled it off over his head. I slid forward in the chair and ran my hands over his hard stomach, then down to the buttons of his jeans. As I worked on the buttons I leaned in and kissed his stomach, ran my tongue over it. Then I tugged his jeans and his boxers down and moved off the chair onto my knees.

I'd never known what it was like to feel this way—wild about someone, nearly out of my mind. I would go crazy if Dex Riggs wasn't mine. He'd gone down on me so many times, but we hadn't done this yet. It was time. I took the head of his cock in my mouth, running my tongue over it. Then I relaxed my jaw and took him deep.

His hands moved into my hair, the strands tangling over his fingers, tugging my scalp. He didn't push me—he just held on, sucking in a breath as I found a rhythm, as I tasted him. When I gave extra attention to the head of his cock he flinched, his stomach muscles tightening. When I used my tongue as I sucked him his breath went harsh and his hands tightened in my hair, as if he liked what I was doing. I was greedy for every detail, and I used everything against him without mercy, my fingers digging into the thighs of his jeans.

I could feel him losing control piece by piece, the tension tightening in him, the pulse under his skin. Finally he pulled me back, sucking in a breath as if it pained him. I looked up at him and saw him watching me, his eyes dark.

"I want to come in your mouth, Lauren," he said roughly. "I'm so fucking close. But we don't make a baby that way. Get on the bed."

I got up and stripped the last of my clothes off, and he did the same. As I lay on the bed Dex came on top of me, all hot, smooth muscles and fragrant skin. He was all business now, worked up and hard. He pinned one wrist above my head with one hand, and he took my other hand in the other and put it between my legs. "Knees up," he said, and as I lifted my knees to his shoulders he shoved into me. "We do it this way," he said and started to move, while both of us worked my clit.

I came on the fifth stroke. The intensity took me by surprise and I cried out, trying to move beneath him as he pinned me down. He thrust deep into me and came too, his hand letting mine go.

This was what I wanted. Just Dex. Nothing else.

And I had a feeling I finally had him.

SEVENTEEN

Dex

SHE STAYED. After I'd screwed up, and after the shit I'd pulled, Lauren stayed. We cleaned up and had something to eat, me wearing boxers and a T-shirt, her wearing panties and one of my shirts. She drank half my orange juice and dug an unused toothbrush out of my bathroom drawer. She stayed.

There was no date with Cindy, of course. I'd ignored her texts just like I'd ignored all the others. There also was no booze or weed in the guest house. She was right about everything.

It was a little unsettling, having a woman who could see through you so easily. I liked it.

For the first time I pulled the blind aside and looked out the window, seeing Luke and Emily's cars in the driveway of the main house. Lauren's car was also there, parked next to mine. "We're busted," I said, dropping the blind again. "The news will be everywhere by morning, if it isn't already."

"I don't care," Lauren said, running her fingers through her hair, untangling some of the strands. "People can talk. I'll deal with it." She picked up my phone from the floor, where it had landed when she threw it, and held it out to me. "Do you want this back?"

I took it and dropped it on the nightstand, watching her expression carefully. "I didn't mean any of that shit I said," I told her.

"Okay," she said, detangling her hair again.

Shit. What had I said about fucking someone else? I was so focused on getting her to hate me and leave, I'd said whatever came into my mind. I made myself say it—and it was hard, because I didn't think I'd ever said the words in my life. "I'm sorry."

She paused and looked at me. Her eyebrows rose. Then she smiled, one of her real smiles. "You get a free pass, remember? I screwed up, too."

I got in bed, thinking about that. With every woman I'd ever dated, a fight meant we were finished. It meant *fuck this, I'm out of here.* It was the only thing I knew. But twice now we'd had a fight and somehow worked past it. Like what we had was worth working for. It felt a little relationship-like, to be honest.

I lay on my back looking at the ceiling as she got into bed next to me, thinking about that word. *Relationship.* Letting it sink in. I waited for panic, but it didn't come. There was just the usual sense of impending doom because of the call I'd had from Kevin, mixed with the certainty that sooner or later she would dump me. But until that happened, the idea of being in a relationship didn't make me want out.

Actually, I wanted more. A lot more. I was just sure I'd never have it.

"When did you get this?" Lauren asked, pushing up the

sleeve of my tee. She traced her fingers over the ink on my shoulder.

Have No Fear. The only tat I had. The only tat I wanted, really. Other guys had more, but that was mine.

"I got it when I was eighteen," I said. "I stole the money for it." I said that because I had to remind her who I was. I wasn't the good guy in any scenario.

"Why those words?" she asked, her fingers tracing them again.

"They're my creed," I said. "The only words I live by. I learned early on not to be afraid of my father. I hated him, but I wasn't afraid of him. Teachers, cops, bosses—I'm not afraid of them either. When I was a cop there were a lot of things I hated about it, but nothing that scared me, no matter what I saw. It's why people think I'm crazy. Maybe I am. I don't really know. But people think there's something wrong with you if you're not afraid."

"So if someone is a jerk to me, you're the person I should call," she said.

"Sure," I replied. "No one messes with my girl."

She leaned in, her hand curled over my shoulder. Her voice was getting sleepier. "You just called me your girl."

I had. I waited for the panic, but it still didn't come. Instead I said, "Once word gets out about us, your mother will know. Does that bother you?"

Lauren sighed, her breath warming the fabric of my T-shirt. "My mother is a cop, but she's not an asshole. You haven't been committing any crimes, have you?"

"No, ma'am," I said.

"Then you'll be fine. Besides, she's had time to get used to Luke. I think she even likes him."

I thought of the phone calls I'd gotten, the problems coming my way. "She might never like me, Parker."

"If that's what she decides, then that's too bad," she said in that kickass way of hers. "You're going to be the father of her grandkid. I'm a grown woman, Dex. I love my mother, but she doesn't run my life. I do."

I touched her arm, ran my fingers over her soft skin. "Listen," I said. "It's you and me, all right? I want you to fucking know that. Everything else is noise that doesn't matter. Whatever happens, it's you and me."

She pressed closer, her body settling sleepily against mine. "You and me," she agreed.

"You got that?"

"I got it."

My fingers touched her wrist. I could feel her pulse there, just under the skin. She was going to be the mother of my kid. She was the only person who mattered.

Minutes later, she fell asleep. But I stayed awake for a long time, staring into the darkness with her pulse against mine.

EIGHTEEN

Dex

"YOU KNOW, if I didn't like women so much," Ryan said, "I'd say this car was as beautiful as one."

We were standing in the bay at Riggs Auto Two, looking at our prized possession. The Porsche was like a movie star who was aging: Time could take its toll, but she was still incredibly gorgeous. To us, anyway.

"Don't let Kate hear you say that," I said.

He sighed. "She knows I'm in lust with this car. She also likes the money this guy is paying us. It's going to float the first part of our year."

I wiped my hands on a rag from my back pocket. "Imagine being so rich you can lay down this much money on a car that doesn't run."

"It'll run," Ryan said. "And when it does... oh, man. Kate's going to need a hazmat suit. I'll probably be turned on for a month."

"TMI, dickface," I said.

"Deal with it." He took out his own grease rag, though he wasn't all that dirty. Even when he was working on cars all day in a dingy garage, he still looked like a guy who made women do double-takes. The asshole. He glanced at me. "You know the grapevine is going crazy about you and Lauren, right?"

Of course I knew. It was three days since she'd come to the guest house, and I knew there was a lot of gossip. Lauren was probably getting most of it. Not a lot of people—except for my brother—had the death wish to actually talk to me. "I have no idea what you're talking about," I said.

Ryan grinned in that good-looking way he had that made me want to give him a Dexbleed, one of my signature punches. "She was at your place *all night*. Luke and Emily both saw it."

"We're friends," I said.

He shook his head. "I just hope you know what you're doing."

Now I was annoyed. "You think I'd play games with Lauren Parker?"

"I don't, actually." He walked over to the hoodie he'd left draped on a chair and shrugged it on. "Neither one of you is the kind to play games. That's why no one can figure out what the hell is happening with you two."

I didn't mean to say it. But I was fucking tired, and it was the only thing I thought about lately. "She wants a baby," I said.

Ryan went very still, his hand on the hoodie's zipper.

I ran a hand through my hair. "Okay? She tried for two years while she was married to Vic VapoRub, and it didn't happen. Now he's out of the picture and she still wants one. She told me about it and I offered to step up. That's what's happening."

"Ah," Ryan said, as if he was figuring it out. "That's why both of you weren't drinking at Jace's birthday."

"No drinking, no weed," I said. "Apparently it helps."

He looked briefly confused, because he had been drunk as hell when he knocked up the girl who had his son, Dylan. But I remembered what Lauren had said, that it was easier for some women than it was for others. "Okay," he said agreeably, zipping his hoodie the rest of the way. "Well, that's noble of you, Dex. Sleeping with a gorgeous woman for the good of humankind."

I shrugged. "She asked."

He smiled. "Lauren is a good person. I hope she gets what she wants. She deserves it. And she'd make a fantastic mother."

"That's it?" I couldn't believe there was no ribbing, no insults. "You have nothing else to say?"

"Not really. Good luck."

Who was this person, and what had he done with my smartass brother? "Don't repeat this, even to Kate," I said. "We're on pins and needles as it is. Lauren doesn't want a whole host of family breathing down her neck, asking if it's happened yet. It stresses her out. If you say anything, you're going to be in a lot of fucking pain."

An expression crossed his face that looked almost like approval. "Protective, I see. You like her."

"Of course I like her. I wouldn't knock up a woman I didn't like. No offense."

"None taken. And I don't mean that you just like her. You really like her."

I opened my mouth—to say what, I had no idea—when we heard the sound of car engines outside. Two of them.

"Saved by the customers," Ryan said.

But they weren't customers. I knew it in my gut. Those two cars pulling in together, the car doors slamming, the sound of more than one person coming to the garage's front door. Customers didn't show up in groups.

But cops did.

The door opened and four men came in. They were plain clothes, which surprised me a little. I didn't think I warranted plainclothes. If I had to guess, I thought they'd send regular old beat cops to do this.

All four were wearing wool coats and identical serious expressions. "Good afternoon," one of them said, though it wasn't a good afternoon at all. "Which one of you is Dexter Riggs?"

"Jesus Christ," Ryan murmured.

"I am," I said. I picked up my coat and put it on.

"We'd like to talk to you about the police raid at Stonehaven Farms last year," the man said. He pulled a piece of paper from his pocket. "We know you've been reluctant to talk, so we have a subpoena."

I waved it away. "Fuck your subpoena."

"Mr. Riggs, this is serious. I suggest you start taking it that way."

I laughed. Felt in my pockets to make sure I had my wallet, my phone. I was going to need them. "Believe me, I take it seriously. You've never seen anyone taking anything as fucking seriously as I take this."

"So you'll come with us?"

"So you can sit me down in a little room and sweat me for hours? Who could say no to that? Yes, I'm coming. You don't need to pull the Al Capone shit."

"Dex," Ryan said, "what the fuck is going on?"

"You always wanted to know what happened when I was on the Detroit PD," I told him. "Now you'll find out." One of the men tried to take my arm, and I shook him off. But when they opened the door again, I followed them.

Tick tock.

It was finally time.

NINETEEN

Dex

"LISTEN TO ME," the cop said to me six hours later. We were in a windowless room in the bowels of a government building in Detroit, but I knew that outside the sky was dark and night had fallen. We would be here all night. "We've arrested Chris Preakness and Johnny Black on criminal charges. Do you understand?"

I understood. Preakness and Black were former colleagues of mine, cops on the Detroit PD. The fact that they were arrested—not just suspended, not just under suspicion—meant that the investigation had gone past the force's internal affairs division and up the line to the county and the state. These guys had identified themselves as state investigators, the kind who weren't called in unless something was big and explosive. The kind of case that would go crazy in the news and be all over the streets.

Two cops arrested on corruption and murder charges was that kind of case.

Next to me, Kevin Blanchard leaned forward in his chair. I'd finally given in and called in the lawyer, even though I didn't like him. He hadn't mentioned the four-thousand-dollar retainer, and I had the feeling he wanted this case—and the publicity—bad enough to overlook that for a little while.

"My client is aware of what's happening," Kevin said, even though that was a blatant lie. "That still doesn't mean he has anything to tell you about either man."

"*Your client* was one of the cops at the Stonehaven Farms bust," the state investigator—Ed Bruce was his name, one of those guys with two first names—said. "He worked closely with both Preakness and Black. He was a witness to everything that went down that night. He can give a full statement, testify in court against Preakness and Black, and seal this case."

"Considering my client's partner was murdered shortly after the bust, and considering he's had death threats himself, he isn't very motivated to testify," Kevin said.

Bruce turned back to me, making eye contact. This was a cop tactic—ignore the lawyer and speak directly to the person you want to question, establishing one-on-one contact. Make your subject feel like the two of you are the only ones in the room.

I looked back at him calmly. "It must be hard, questioning cops," I said. "We know all your tricks."

"Dex, stop talking," Kevin said.

Bruce ignored both of us, because he was good. "You need to make a statement," he said to me with sincerity—another questioning trick. "If you don't, we can make a case that you were complicit in the corruption in the Stonehaven case. And instead of going free, you go down with them."

"So you're saying I have to either turn on my fellow cops or go to jail."

"That's one way of interpreting your situation, yes."

"And if I testify, I get killed. So really my choices are death or jail. Do I have that right?"

"No one's going to kill you," the other investigator said. He was standing back, behind Bruce, leaning against the wall. The wool coats were gone and both men were in suits, their ties loosened after the first hour of questioning. "We have both men in custody, and their request for bail was denied. They're staying where they are until the trial."

"And if they aren't convicted, they walk out the door of the courthouse. And put a bullet in my head."

It was hard to take, that I was saying that about two cops I had worked with. It was a hard thing to believe. But I had seen Preakness and Black in action the night of the Stonehaven raid, and my partner was dead over it. I knew they would do it. I absolutely knew.

Death or jail. What a fucking choice. No wonder I had run from it for so long. No wonder I had barely slept for as long as I could remember.

Have No Fear.

"Riggs," Bruce said, playing Good Cop. The Good Cop/Bad Cop thing actually worked if you did it right. "No one thinks you actually took part in taking the drugs and the money. No one thinks you're the guy who put a bullet in someone's head. You had a good record and a good reputation."

I laughed.

"Okay, there were a few behavioral infractions on your record," Bruce said, still doing Good Cop. "You have a hard time with rules. But those are minor in the scheme of things. You were a good cop. And you had an alibi when your partner was killed, so we know you didn't do it."

"My partner was killed because of me," I said.

It was true. After the Stonehaven raid, my partner and I had argued. Rick wanted to go straight up the line and report it. I thought that was dangerous. Preakness and Black caught wind of what we were thinking, and the next thing I knew, Rick was gunned down in a drive-by as he got out of his car. The gunman was never found. And I'd had a warning from Preakness: *Shut up or his wife and kids are next.*

I'd shut up.

If I'd followed what Rick wanted from the first, maybe it would have been different. Maybe he'd still be alive. But then again, maybe not. I'd never fucking know.

"Here's what I think," Bruce said. "You're not talking because you're protecting someone. But I don't think the person you're protecting is yourself. After the Stonehaven raid, after your partner died, you quit the force. A few months after that, you left town. You wouldn't have done that if Preakness and Black were protecting you. Those aren't the actions of someone who has their backing. They're the actions of someone who's been threatened. And yet you were brave a dozen times while you worked Vice. You faced guys a lot worse than Preakness and Black and you didn't break a sweat. So what did they threaten that made you leave?"

I was silent.

"Here's the other thing I think," Bruce said. "If we don't nail these guys, if you don't testify—because believe me, if your testimony is what I think it is then it will nail them—then the threat never goes away. You live with it forever. And maybe you haven't had a lot of choice up until now, but now it's different. Now, if you want to live under a cloud for the rest of your life, that's your call."

I thought about Rick, his wife and kids. Rick's funeral. The two bodies at the Stonehaven site. I thought of Lauren and the baby. My brothers back in Westlake. Their girlfriends. Our business.

A life. A real one.

Bruce was right. It was my call. I had tried to push Lauren away, and it hadn't worked. If she had a baby—my baby—I'd never push her away again.

But if I did this wrong, she would push me away. Maybe not tomorrow, but someday. Because I wouldn't be worthy of her, and I wouldn't be worthy of being a father.

I had to be someone better, and it had to start now.

I looked Bruce in the eye, matching him cop trick for cop trick. "Listen up," I said. "Here's what happened."

"Dex," Kevin said.

"We were set to do a raid," I said. "Me and Rick, Preakness and Black. We'd been following the trail of a big dealer. Coke, meth, fentanyl—he dealt all of it at one time or another. A one-stop shop, if you will. We had a tip that he was hiding out with his stash at a farm called Stonehaven, outside of the city. The four of us were to go in. The usual procedure for a bust like that is more than four men, but at the last minute Preakness and Black cancelled the others who were supposed to go. That should have tipped me off."

"Dex," Kevin said again. I held my hand up and he shut up.

"Go on," Bruce said.

"We got to the farmhouse at dusk. It was a shit show. We went in by the book as if there was an army in there, but there was no one. Just two guys in the house, both of them high as fuck. They were stumbling around, shouting, barely coherent. The whole place stank. One of the guys pulled a gun and Rick and I were distracted, disarming him and getting him subdued."

Bruce's face was stony, because both of those junkies had ended up dead that night. Everyone in the room knew it.

"Preakness and Black went upstairs," I continued. "They came back down and said the house was clear—the guys we were looking for weren't here. There were no drugs, no weapons cache, no nothing. Just these two head cases who barely knew where they were. The whole place had been cleaned out. They sent Rick and me to check the basement."

Bruce glanced back at his partner, then looked back at me. I knew this whole session was being recorded; they'd told me from the start. They would have every word on record.

"What then?" Bruce asked.

"We checked the basement. There was no one there. While we were down there, we heard two gunshots upstairs. We came back up to find both junkies dead and Preakness with a gun in his hand. He said the junkies had rushed him with weapons, but we didn't see any fucking weapons. Also, Preakness didn't use his service weapon in his supposed self-defense. He had another gun on him, an unregistered one. He told us he didn't want the paperwork over a couple of junkies, and we'd just blame the deaths on one of the dealers we were looking for."

My head hurt. My bones hurt. Jesus, even my eyes hurt. I rubbed my forehead. I had to get the rest of this story out. So I kept talking.

"Preakness and Black said it was time to leave. Rick and I didn't have much choice but to follow. Preakness took the gun— he must have ditched it somewhere. To this day, I don't really know why he killed those junkies. They must have known something he didn't want repeated. We'll never know what it is now. The only thing I knew was that he killed them and he didn't hesitate.

"I went outside and Black was loading duffel bags into the back of his car. He'd taken his own car instead of one of the fleet, because he said it was better for undercover ops. And he was just standing there right in front of me, loading bags into his fucking car. I asked him what he was doing, and he looked right in my face the way you're looking now. He said, 'If you say you saw this, your partner is fucking dead. Write up the report, Riggs, and make it clean.'"

"Did Rick see Black loading his car, too?"

"Yes, he did. He was out of earshot so he didn't hear what Black said about killing him. To Rick, it was straightforward. Preakness and Black were dirty cops; it was a dirty raid. People were dead. He wasn't a dirty cop. So his job was to report it, to stamp it out. He didn't see it any other way."

"So you tried to talk him out of it," Bruce said.

I ran a hand through my hair. My muscles ached and I had cold sweat on my back, like I was coming down with something— except I knew I wasn't. Telling this story was making me feel sick. "I didn't want to tell him about the threat. I didn't want to scare him. I thought we should think it over, make sure it was a safe move to turn on Preakness and Black. Make sure we had all of our evidence in line. We had to file the official report, and the instructions were clear: We were supposed to lie. We were supposed to say we went out to the farmhouse on a tip and there was nothing there but two dead junkies. One page, file it away, move on. Rick wanted to tell the truth. We argued. And then he was dead." I rubbed the back of my neck. My partner had been gunned down when he got out of his car to go to the hardware store on a Tuesday afternoon. He was supposed to fix a broken water heater at his house, and when he'd gone to the hardware store—boom. It was over.

"We have the guy who did that hit," Bruce said. "We have his statement that it was on Preakness's orders. He's agreed to testify in court. What we don't know is why. We also have no other witnesses to the murder of the two junkies." He leaned forward again. "Your testimony, Riggs, will send both of those guys down for a very long time."

"That isn't good enough," I said.

Bruce raised his eyebrows. Next to me, Kevin said, "Dex, we need to talk in private."

I ignored him. "After Rick died, Black warned me that Rick's wife and kids were next if I didn't keep my mouth shut."

"Can you prove that?"

"Of course I can't fucking prove it. Why do you think I gave in?"

Bruce turned in his chair and looked at his partner. His partner left the room.

"We'll pick them up," Bruce said, turning back to me. "We'll put them somewhere safe until the trial's over."

"And then what?"

"And then we put Preakness and Black away and they don't have to worry anymore. But only if you help us."

I swallowed. Was this really possible? Could I get rid of the poison I'd swallowed, that ate me up every day? Bruce was an asshole, but he was right. There was only one way. It was either do this or spend the rest of my life being someone I didn't want to be anymore.

"All right," I said. "If you can keep them safe, I'll testify."

"My client needs protection, too," Kevin said. "It's clear his life is in danger over this. He can't just be released to go home."

"Wait a second." I turned to him. "I never said I wanted that. I'm a trained cop. I can handle myself."

"Rick was a trained cop, too," Kevin said. "You need protection."

"Fuck no. I said what you wanted. I'll make a full statement. I'll agree to testify. Then I'm going home."

"No way," Bruce said, agreeing with Kevin. "Is that what you want, Riggs? To get shot when you get out of your car? No offense, but if that happens my case goes straight down the drain. And I've been working to nail these guys for almost a year. I've never seen two more corrupt cops in my life."

"I'm not under arrest, so you can't keep me," I said.

"Yes, I can. You're going to one of our safe houses. No one

will know where you are, you'll be guarded twenty-four-seven, and your phone privileges will be restricted. No one comes or goes. That's final until the trial is over."

I stared at him. "And when is the trial?"

"Three weeks."

"You want me to go sit in a room by myself for three weeks while no one knows where I am? Are you fucking kidding me?"

"I'd never kid about this, Riggs, and I'm not starting now."

Three weeks. Three weeks to keep me safe, and then this would be over. I'd been living with this for years, letting it drag me down. I could finish this once and for all. Three weeks wasn't a very long time in the scheme of things. It shouldn't matter.

But the first thing I thought was, *Lauren will know if she's pregnant in three weeks.*

I looked at Bruce's face, looked into his eyes. Hard as granite. The might of the state and the U.S. government on his side. "I don't have a choice, do I?" I said.

His expression didn't flicker. "Not even a little bit," he replied. "We should have warned you to pack a bag."

TWENTY

Lauren

"I DON'T GET IT," I said. "Where is he?"

I was standing in line at Westlake's lone independent coffee shop with Kate. She had taken a lease on a space a block away for her new tutoring business, and I'd helped her inspect the place before signing the paperwork. I hadn't seen Dex in two weeks. He hadn't called me. He hadn't called anyone. Since the day Ryan watched Dex get taken away, he'd pretty much disappeared.

"Haven't you been watching the news?" Kate said. She was wearing a thick sweater with a down vest zipped over it, her red hair twisted up from her neck. The bone-chilling frigid weather had let up for a day, and the snow outside was melting into slush. "The trial of those two cops is all over the news. The defense attorney petitioned for a media blackout and was denied. It's going to be a circus."

"I know," I said as we moved up a step. Two cops going on trial for corruption and murder, including murder of one of their own, was the biggest story in Detroit right now. "What I don't know is what it has to do with Dex. Or why those cops took him away. Or where he actually is." We moved nearer the front, and I dug in my purse for my wallet. "Is he in a hotel? A hospital? A jail cell? A locked room somewhere? Why hasn't he come home or called anyone? We don't even know if he's okay."

Kate's expression was sympathetic as she listened to my fretting. "He's sequestered until after the trial. They told us that much."

"That's no information at all. It's nothing." I exhaled a frustrated breath. "He wasn't even allowed to pack anything. It's like he just disappeared."

Kate sighed as we stepped up to the register. "I know what you mean. I'd be beside myself if Ryan vanished for weeks without being able to call."

I didn't answer that. She was equating me and Dex to her and Ryan, who were officially a couple. Dex and I weren't officially a couple, but apparently no one believed that anymore. Not after I spent the night at the guest house, my car parked outside.

It felt like we were a couple. *You and me,* Dex had said. *Nothing else matters.* And then he was gone.

If they were hiding Dex before the trial, it must mean he was in danger.

And maybe I was pregnant. I still didn't know.

I was at the point where I could take a pregnancy test, but I didn't want to. I wanted to take the test when Dex was with me to see the results—something I realized only after he'd vanished into thin air.

Where the hell was he?

We ordered our drinks—mine was herbal tea, which Kate didn't comment on—and walked toward the door. I wanted to tell

Kate everything. I wanted to unburden myself of the secrets I was carrying around. I wanted to ask her what she thought I should do.

Then I remembered what it was like to find out I wasn't pregnant—again. I'd been through it so many times. I couldn't handle the sympathetic looks, the attempts to cheer me up. *You're young. You can always try again!* People meant well, but nothing made it any easier.

Dex was the only person I could talk to, and I'd lost him.

"Ryan thinks Dex is going to testify against those cops," Kate said as she pushed the door open. "There are rumors that Dex is dirty, too, that he's testifying so he won't be prosecuted. But I don't think that's true."

"It isn't true," I said, thinking of that last night I saw Dex. How I'd challenged him to tell me he was corrupt, and he hadn't been able to say it. I always knew when Dex was lying, and in that moment he hadn't been able to lie to me.

No, it was something else tearing him apart that night. Something he hadn't told me.

"What if they don't convict them?" I said, forcing my deepest fear out into words. "What if they go through the whole trial and get a Not Guilty verdict? What then?" If he testified against those men and they walked free, would Dex even be safe?

What hadn't he told me about his career as a cop?

"They'll convict them," Kate said. "They have to, right?"

I didn't know. I pulled out my keys. "What are you going to do now?"

Kate sighed. "I'm going back to my computer to go over the budget one more time. Then I have a call with the graphic designer about the marketing materials."

I smiled at her. A year ago, Kate had had no idea what she wanted to do with her life. She'd taken a job as nanny to Ryan's son Dylan and—it was so juicy—she'd fallen for her boss. Since she was pretty much Dylan's stepmom now and not his nanny, she'd found a passion for tutoring kids who needed help with their grades. Her new tutoring school, which we'd just signed the lease for, was going to open in a month. "You're doing good," I told her. "Remember, it's a marathon. This is going to be great."

"Thanks to you," she said, smiling back. "I'd have been lost without your help, Lauren. Seriously."

"You can pay me by being a reference for all of my new consulting clients."

"I will."

"Lauren!"

I turned, scanning the sidewalk. It was Vic. He was walking toward me, and he didn't look happy. I couldn't think of why, since I hadn't talked to him in weeks.

"Is that the ex?" Kate whispered.

I nodded. "Vic," I said when he came closer. I looked around. "Where's Shannon?"

He ignored that. He was really in a mood about something. "Dex Riggs?" he said, glaring at me and not even looking at Kate. "Of all the guys in Westlake, you're dating *Dex Riggs?*"

I felt my spine go straight. I looked my ex-husband up and down: jeans, boots, that stupid zip-up puffy coat he'd refused to get rid of every winter. *It cost a hundred dollars!* he'd say every time I suggested giving it away. And the ugly coat would go back in the closet so it would look terrible on him for yet another year.

He'd had a haircut recently, and since he was wearing no hat, his ears were red. I wondered if Shannon had made him get a haircut. I really didn't care.

"Does that bother you?" I asked him.

"Bother me?" He said this as if I'd asked something outrageous. "What the fuck are you thinking, Lauren? Have you lost your mind?"

I narrowed my eyes at him. "That's what has you all worked

up? Me dating someone else? You've been with Shannon for months. She freaking lives with you."

"Not someone else," Vic said. "Dex Riggs. A guy you would never give the time of day to in high school."

Yes, I would have, if I'd taken a chance. And I should have. "We're not in high school anymore, Vic. We haven't been for a while. Besides, how do you know who I'm dating?"

"Everyone knows!" He waved his gloved hands. "Everyone who went to Westlake High has heard it. Lauren Parker is dating a Riggs brother. Not just any Riggs brother—the worst one, the crazy one. The one who's apparently a corrupt cop."

"He isn't a corrupt cop," I snapped. "And people should mind their own business."

"You're defending him?" Vic said. "What is this, Lauren? Are you depressed or something? Are you trying to be rebellious? Are you trying to get back at me?"

"I'm not doing any of those things!" I shouted. People around us were starting to look. "Get over yourself."

"You were always so smart and level-headed," Vic said. "You'd never waste yourself on a piece of shit like Dex Riggs. At least, that's what I thought. Maybe I didn't know you at all."

I had a strange, out-of-body experience in that moment. I'd known the man in front of me since I was sixteen. He wasn't my first kiss—that was Dex—but he was my first everything else. The first man I'd slept with. The first man I'd tried to have a baby with. The only man I'd said *I love you* to, the only man I'd married, and the only man I'd divorced.

So much of my life, to date, was wrapped up in Vic Voorhees. And as I stood there on a slushy sidewalk, holding my forgotten cup of tea, I realized he was right.

"You don't know me," I told him. "You never did. I don't know whose fault that is. Maybe yours, or maybe mine. But you don't know me at all."

"That's bullshit," Vic said. "We were married."

"So what?" I said. "You know my birthday, when I remind you. You know I run a business. You know what I like for breakfast. You know I hate flying and Christmas shopping and that I have ten kinds of lip gloss. But that isn't *knowing* me, Vic. Not even close."

Vic rolled his eyes, as if none of that mattered. "So what? Dex Riggs knows you?"

It's you and me, Dex had said. *Everything else is noise that doesn't matter. Whatever happens, it's you and me.*

"Yeah," I said to my former husband. "He knows me."

"That's bullshit. I don't know what's gotten into you, Lauren. You must be desperate."

I opened my mouth to say something, but there was a *whoosh* sound and a snowball hit Vic's face, exploding in white. I turned and saw that Kate had put her coffee down and was scooping up more snow into her mittened hands.

"Leave her alone," she said to Vic. "You're upsetting her."

Vic brushed snow off his face and gaped at her. "Who the hell are you?"

"I'm Lauren's friend," Kate said. "Oh, and I'm the girlfriend of another Riggs brother. You, know, Ryan. The good-looking one you probably hated all through high school."

"What the fuck?" Vic said.

"You're bothering Lauren," Kate said, tapping her snowball into a sphere. "Go away." She aimed and threw again. Vic tried to duck, but the snowball still hit him in the shoulder, the snow spraying onto the side of his neck.

"Oh, my God," I said in awe. "Kate, your aim."

"Try it," she replied. "It's fun."

I put my tea down on the roof of my car and picked up some snow.

"Don't pack it too hard," Kate said. "When you pack it loose, it really explodes."

Vic brushed the snow off him and glared at me. "Lauren, people are watching. You're insane."

"Then throw one back," I said, packing my snowball nice and round.

"You've lost your mind."

I sighed. "Kate is right, you're bothering me. You're not in my life anymore. Dex is. If you want to accost me on the street and insult him, you're getting a snowball."

"You're actually defending that asshole?"

I whipped the snowball at him and got him right at the base of his throat, hitting his ugly coat. The snow sprayed upward into his face. Kate threw hers and got him square in the chest.

Vic could have laughed it off. He could have thrown one back. He could have graciously admitted defeat. Instead he just stood there, getting redder and redder, angrier and angrier, and I knew deep in my bones that leaving him had been the right choice. It came over me like a wash of relief. *Thank God I don't have to go home with him and listen to him complain. Thank God I kept my own last name. Thank God he's not my problem anymore.*

"I'm leaving," he said, sounding less mature than Ryan's seven-year-old son.

"Thank fucking God," I said.

"Profanity, too," Vic observed, turning away. "Dex Riggs is a good influence on you, I can see."

We pelted his back with snowballs as he retreated.

When Vic was out of range, Kate brushed the snow off her mittens. "That was weird," she said. "It was funny and sort of sad at the same time."

I shook my head. She was right. It was funny, but it was also Vic to a T. Joyless and humorless and without even a hint of self-awareness. "I married the wrong person," I said as I watched his car drive away. "There's nothing I can do about it now."

"You get the right person, and you hold on to him," Kate said. "That's what you can do. Even if he's a Riggs brother. I wouldn't trade my Riggs brother for anything. And anyone who wants to insult Ryan has to deal with me."

I turned and looked at her—her chin up, her fierce red hair. A few weeks ago, I hadn't had any friends. I had a feeling that was changing. "Thanks," I said.

Kate smiled at me. "You're welcome. But our drinks got cold. I say we go in and get new ones."

TWENTY-ONE

Dex

SINCE I'D NEVER BEEN SEQUESTERED by the State of Michigan before, I had no idea what to expect. What I got was a room at a Howard Johnson's.

We were somewhere near the Detroit Metro Airport, hiding in plain sight in a sea of bland hotels. My room was on the twelfth floor. From early morning to the middle of the night I listened to planes take off and land outside my window. I could see the blinking lights of the runways in the dark. I looked at them a lot, because there wasn't much else to look at.

I was guarded twenty-four-seven. They couldn't put cops on me all the time—I knew the Detroit PD, and they didn't have the budget for that. Besides, cops had real work to do. So I was watched over by security guards who worked for a contract company. I wasn't under arrest, but since they didn't want me walking away, they gave me a security guard for a roommate in rotating shifts. To put it mildly, it was fucking awkward.

Today's security guard was named Andre. He sat in one of the hotel room chairs, scrolling on his phone, his big bulk slumped. I lay on top of the made bed, fully dressed, my hands laced behind my head on the pillow. The TV in the room was on, tuned to a cable news channel, but neither of us was watching.

"How about a drive?" I said. "Just to see what's going on in the world."

"No," Andre said.

"Can I order more room service?"

"No."

"How about a newspaper? They must have one somewhere."

Andre briefly glanced up from his phone and looked at me. "You're already watching the news."

I sighed and scratched my stomach. They hadn't let me go home and get my things, so I had new clothes courtesy of the Michigan taxpayers: two button-down shirts, one pair of jeans, six pairs of socks, and six pairs of underwear. Since I'd been here for two and a half weeks, I'd had to use the hotel laundry service. I'd also been issued a toothbrush, toothpaste, a comb, a stick of deodorant, and a razor. Also on the taxpayer's tab.

It was a little like prison, except more comfortable and with room service. I did situps and pushups to burn energy. I got regular visits from investigators and lawyers, going over my upcoming testimony. We'd rehearsed it backward and forward. I'd been given a pre-trial haircut—performed by a barber brought to the hotel—so I wouldn't look like a bum on the stand.

They'd taken my phone on that first day and they hadn't given it back. That was the worst thing. They didn't want anyone using the phone's GPS to track me, and they didn't want me calling anyone and telling them where I was. They'd unplugged the room's landline, too. The only person in the room with a phone was Andre, which meant when I wanted room service I had to ask him to call for me.

I was losing my fucking mind. Partly because of the trial, but mostly because of Lauren. They'd taken my phone with her calendar on it, but I knew the dates by heart. I couldn't believe it either, but I knew a woman's cycle like I knew my own name. And her cycle said that by now she was either pregnant or she wasn't.

I had to know.

It was against the rules, but rules had never stopped me before.

"Andre," I said, still lying on my back looking at the ceiling, "there's a problem I need to point out."

He glanced up from his phone and raised an eyebrow at me. He was big, black, and at least two hundred and twenty pounds. The raised-eyebrow look was a little menacing.

"The trial is coming up, and I don't have a suit," I said. "I should be wearing a suit and tie, shouldn't I?"

He didn't say anything, but he scowled a little, so I knew I was right.

"They don't have to buy me one," I said. "I have a perfectly good suit and tie sitting at home. New shoes, too. My brother just got married and I was best man."

Andre's gaze cut to the room's closet, which we both knew had no suit in it. "We'll get you a suit," he said. "I'll make a call."

"The wedding suit is already altered. It fits me perfectly. I had the whole thing dry cleaned after the wedding was over. One of my brothers could just grab it out of the closet in my place, put it in a bag, and hand it over."

I knew how this worked by now. If they didn't use my suit, then someone had to go buy me one. They'd have to take measurements, match shirts and ties, the whole thing. What I was offering was much easier.

"Which brother should we contact?" Andre asked.

"Any of them could do it. But Luke already has a key to my place."

He sighed and levered his bulk up from his chair. "I'll be right back. Don't move." He left the room and went into the hallway, where I heard him talking on the phone.

BY DINNERTIME I had the suit. A lackey had been sent to meet Luke to pick it up, without giving away where I was of course. Luke had folded the whole thing and stuffed it in a grocery bag because he was an asshole. I thanked Andre and went to the closet, where I started to hang everything up.

It wasn't in the jacket—too obvious. It wasn't in the pants. But when I got to the shoes, I hit the jackpot. Luke knew perfectly well what little goodie to send me. When I bent and put the shoes in the closet, I upended one of them and shook out the small burner phone he'd stuffed in the toe.

I put the phone in my jeans pocket and walked to the TV, turning the sound up a notch. Andre was staring at his phone and didn't seem to notice. I went into the bathroom, locked the door, and turned on the tap.

Then I called Lauren.

She answered on the first ring. "Dex?" Someone had obviously told her what was up.

I'd never been so glad to hear anyone's voice in my life. "Parker," I said, moving to the back of the bathroom so Andre wouldn't hear me.

"Are you okay?"

"I'm fine. I'm stuffed in a hotel room with security watching over me, but I'm fine."

"You're going to testify." Her voice was tight with worry.

"Yeah." I took a breath. Telling her was going to be harder than telling the lawyers, the court, anyone. "Listen. I was on a raid with my partner and some very crooked cops on the take. They killed witnesses and took money and drugs. They told my partner and me to shut up or else."

She was silent, but I heard her intake of breath.

"We wanted to do the right thing," I said. "Rick and me both. He wanted to do it right away and I wanted to wait. So we hesitated, which was my fault. And the next thing I knew, my partner was gunned down in a drive-by."

"Oh my God, Dex," Lauren said softly.

I kept talking. "The other cops said they'd go after my partner's wife and kids next if I didn't fall in line. Which meant writing up a normal police report and keeping my mouth shut." I ran a hand through my hair. "I didn't know what to do, but in the end I had to make a choice. I wrote the report. I kept my mouth shut. They got off with no consequences and kept doing what they were doing. No one reported a goddamned thing."

"And it ate you up inside," Lauren said softly. "That's what you meant about a decision that haunts you."

She was dead on. She was always so fucking dead on with me. There was no point denying it. "I couldn't risk them," I said. "I had no doubt they would have killed Rick's wife and kids. But what kind of cops lets his corrupt brothers walk free? I wasn't on the take myself, but I may as well have been. It was going on in my precinct and I didn't stop it. That makes me just as bad as them, as far as I'm concerned."

She let out a breath that sounded like a sigh. "That explains so much. The rumors about you. How you said that all of them were true. Why you've been punishing yourself for so long. Why you tried to push me away the night of Jace's birthday."

Of all the shitty things I'd done in my life, I still felt bad about that one. "I'm sorry," I said. "I should have told you earlier. But these guys don't fuck around. The more people who know anything, the more targets there are. If they were willing to go after Rick's wife and kids—and they were—then I had no way to keep anyone safe."

"Even yourself."

I'd never cared about myself. Not after that night. "That doesn't matter. I'm not a father like Rick was."

"You should be." Her voice cracked, like she'd been holding together with cheap glue that let go. "You were supposed to be. But you're not."

I sagged against the bathroom wall. Outside, I heard Andre saying something, probably asking what was taking so long. "Lauren," I said. "I know the schedule, baby. Are you saying what I think you are?"

Her answer was a gasp of pain, a sound she tried to control in the back of her throat. Instead it came out in a sob.

I knew my answer. I closed my eyes and leaned my forehead against the bathroom wall, bracing a hand there to keep me upright. I felt like my ribs were cracking open. On the other end of the phone, Lauren sobbed again, her heart broken in two.

I banged my palm against the wall. My woman was crying—fucking *sobbing*—and I was stuck here in this shitty room, listening to it on a stolen phone instead of being there for her. "Baby, please," I begged her. "Please don't cry. I'll come home as fast as I can and we'll try again."

"It's me," she said brokenly when she could finally find words. "When I tried before they didn't know...you know...whose fault it was. They did tests but nothing was conclusive. But this has to prove it, right? The problem is me." She heaved a breath. "It's never going to happen. I'll never be a mother no matter what I do."

"Don't say that." The sounds she was making were ripping my heart straight out of my chest. My guts were bleeding on the floor. I always knew this about her, that a baby was a deep part of what she wanted. It wasn't a lark or a hobby or a status symbol. It was part of the person she wanted to be. "You're not even thirty yet. We'll do IVF or IUI"—yeah, I'd researched everything—"or whatever it takes, whatever it costs. And if none of that works, we'll adopt. But you're going to be a mother. We're going to have kids. Do you get me? I'm here with you this whole way, on every part of the ride. I'm not going anywhere and I'm not giving up. We're doing this, Lauren. We are."

Andre knocked on the bathroom door. "I can hear you talking in there, Riggs. I'll break this door down if I have to."

"Dex," Lauren said in a shaky voice, "are you sure? Because I have to tell you, this isn't a very fun ride. I've been on it for a while now and it's already cost me one marriage. I don't think I can survive it if it costs me you, too."

"The guy you married was a fucking lightweight," I said. "That isn't me. He didn't feel one one-hundredth about you that I do. I have no fear, remember? It's my creed. I'm not afraid of this trial, these cops and lawyers. I'm not afraid of doctors or procedures. I'm not afraid of failure, because I've faced it too many times. Failure puts me down but it never puts me out. So I'm going to testify, and I'm going to nail these fucking guys. I'm going to put them down so hard they never see daylight again. And when I'm finished, I'm coming back to Westlake for you. No lawyers or custody agreements. Just you, me, and a baby, however we get there." I lowered my voice so she could hear me over Andre banging on the bathroom door. "It's you and me," I told her. "Always remember that, no matter how bad it gets. It's you and me."

"You and me," Lauren said, her voice a little stronger now. "I love you, Dex."

"I hope so, because when I get out of here I'm coming for you. See you in a couple days."

I hung up and flung open the bathroom door just as Andre was about to kick it. He had his foot raised and everything, his body braced. He looked at me in surprise and I tossed the phone at him.

"I'm done with that," I said. "I'm ready. Let's fucking get this over with."

TWENTY-TWO

Lauren

I WANTED to go to Detroit for the trial, but everyone told me it was a bad idea. The courtroom was closed because the case was so controversial; there were no cameras or video feeds allowed inside. The courthouse itself was packed with media, would-be spectators, and curious onlookers, mixed with security and cops. The whole thing was a circus. Even if I went, I wouldn't be able to see the trial, and I didn't know where Dex was staying. I hadn't heard from Dex again after that one phone call. Luke had given Dex a burner phone, and I assumed it had been taken from him again.

So I waited in Westlake, helpless.

I worked. I consulted with clients. I spent time with Emily and my parents. I sat alone in my apartment, watching TV without seeing it. Inside, I was empty and alone.

I had planned to take a pregnancy test, but Mother Nature decided I didn't need it. I got my period instead, days early, which maybe meant I'd been briefly pregnant—or maybe not. I'd never know now.

The trial lasted a week. The two accused cops claimed they were innocent, that they'd been railroaded. It was soon clear that wasn't the case. There was a lot of evidence against them, which the media covered obsessively. It had caught the public imagination that two cops would execute junkies point-blank, then hire a contract killer to execute a fellow cop, a married father of two, as he got out of his car at the hardware store. The news stories speculated that maybe the killer acted alone, that his claim that he'd been hired was a lie. They speculated about the motive—why would they kill another cop unless they were truly dirty and he'd threatened to expose them? If they weren't dirty, there was no motive.

I tried not to pay attention, but I couldn't help myself. I watched the coverage and read about it every day.

And then, finally, Dex testified in court.

I saw it while I was standing on a cold, snowy street in Westlake, walking past a Best Buy. There was a bank of TVs in the window, and every one of them showed me Dex Riggs.

I stopped dead, my grocery bags forgotten. He was being led out of an official car into the courthouse, surrounded by cops. He was wearing the suit I recognized from Luke and Emily's wedding, and he was clean-shaven, his hair trim. He looked a little pale, but his dark blue eyes blazed. He looked determined and wicked. He looked gorgeous and dangerous and very, very hot. He looked like he was on a mission, and nothing on earth could stop him.

There were dozens of him, of all sizes, plastered over the wall of TVs. He came out of the car with his usual lethal grace, as if none of the hoopla around him even registered. He didn't look at or speak to anyone as he was accompanied through the crowd. Then the newscaster spoke on mute, and the footage looped back to Dex getting out of the car again. They were talking about him, though I couldn't hear what they were saying. The caption at the bottom of the screen said FORMER COP DEXTER RIGGS TO TESTIFY TODAY.

"Damn," said a voice next to me. I turned to see another woman paused on the sidewalk, watching Dex, a knit hat jammed down over her head. "That is one hot man," she commented. "He can arrest me anytime."

"He might be dirty," the woman on the other side of her said.

The woman in the hat laughed. "Oh, he's definitely dirty. At least, he is in my fantasies."

"That's Dex Riggs," the other woman said. "Don't you know him? Everyone does. He's a hometown boy."

"I just moved here," the hat lady said. "But if that's the kind of man you have in Westlake, then I'm staying."

On the TVs, the shot changed to the newscaster again, and then to other things. The women drifted away. I hefted my bags and walked slowly toward my car. I could still see Dex in my mind's eye, the look in his blue eyes, his cheekbones, his clean-shaven jaw. The set of his shoulders as he walked into that courthouse.

No matter what, it's you and me.

When I get out of here, I'm coming for you.

I put my groceries in my car and got in. I'd heard every version of the truth. Dex was a hero; he was a dirty cop; he was brave; he was an untrustworthy liar. He was the kid everyone remembered who got into trouble. His father was a criminal serving time, and yet he was a cop with a flawless record before he quit. He was crazy. He was hot. As a witness, there was no doubt he'd be a loose cannon.

No one saw the Dex I saw, the one with bruises on his neck

like ink smears. No one else had seen the look of pain on his face that night when I'd dared him to tell me he was corrupt.

You and me.

"Dex," I said out loud in the car, my breath frosting in the cold air, "come home."

THE JURY WAS out for three days. Three long, endless days that seemed to stretch for years. Even though Dex had finished testifying—the media called his testimony "devastating"—we still had no word from him. He was probably still under protection in case of a Not Guilty verdict.

I had resorted to helping out at The Big Do to keep myself as busy as possible. Emily knew there was something up with me—she wasn't stupid, and I was pretty obvious—but for once she didn't pry. I didn't get a single demand that I sit down and tell her everything, which was a lot of restraint for her.

We had closed the shop and were tidying up, doing the last-minute things before locking up, when there was a polite knock on the front glass doors. Our mother stood there, peering in and waving at us.

Emily unlocked the door and let her in. "Mom! What's up?"

"I came to see my girls," Mom said. "I heard this is the place to find them."

She unzipped her coat and put it on the customer hook at the front. Our mother had been a Westlake cop for all of her career, first as a beat cop in uniform and then as a sergeant. She'd battled not only bad guys but rampant sexism for her whole career, which made her a hero. Now she was just past fifty and still fit and strong, her hair tied back in its trademark braid down her back. She smiled at both of us.

"You're not working late?" I asked her. Late nights were a staple of Mom's job. Emily and I had never minded it, but now that our parents were divorced we could see that it must have taken a toll on their marriage. Our father had done a lot of the day-to-day stuff when we were kids, and Mom had worked more than one Christmas Eve.

"Not tonight," Mom said, unwinding her scarf. "With this trial on in Detroit everyone is on their best behavior, including every cop on the Westlake PD. I think every guy that works for me is on pins and needles."

She looked at me, and I tried to give her a smile, but it probably wasn't very convincing.

"Okay, so what?" Emily said, twisting her hair back into a ponytail. "Do you guys want to go out for dinner? Drinks?"

"Oh, you two are probably too busy," Mom said, sitting in one of the salon chairs and swiveling it, looking around. "I haven't been to your salon in years, Lauren. It looks great."

"Hey, it's my salon, too," Emily said.

"Yes, it is." Mom used that tone she'd used our whole lives, the tone of a parent of twins who is appeasing both of them. "I just meant that Lauren originally picked this place and decorated it. I don't think I've fully appreciated it. I admit, I thought you were crazy at the time."

"It was crazy," I said, powering down the booking computer at the front desk. "I was only twenty-one. I took all of my savings from working at the mall, and then I made a business plan and went and got a bank loan. If it hadn't worked out, I'd likely be homeless."

"Never," Mom said. "You can always stay with me."

Emily and I exchanged a look. Emily had done that when she came back to town—moved into her childhood bedroom at Mom and Dad's house. Mom was nice enough, but going back to my twin bed with my childhood bookshelf next to it wasn't exactly ideal.

"Well, you should come here more often," Emily said to Mom. "You know we'd do your hair for free. You've had that braid for a long time, Mom. You're single and back on the market now. You should get a new cut and color."

Mom laughed as if that was outrageous. "Oh, no. My braid does just fine, thanks. No fuss, no muss."

That was when it hit me. Mom loved us, but she wasn't a big "drop in just because" person. In fact, I couldn't remember the last time she'd dropped in for no reason. That was because Mom rarely did anything for no reason.

She had a reason she was here.

"What is it, Mom?" I asked her. Because when you were talking to Nora Parker the cop, your best course of action was always to say what you wanted straight out.

"What is what?" Emily asked.

"The reason Mom's here," I said.

Emily narrowed her eyes, then looked at Mom again. "Well?" she asked her.

Mom bit her lip and looked uncomfortable, still swiveling in the chair. "This whole case in Detroit has me thinking about the Riggs brothers."

Emily and I looked at each other. Em's eyes were wide.

"Those boys were always trouble," Mom continued. "It wasn't their fault, really. They had no mother. They only had Mike Riggs, who was just about the worst father anyone could imagine. So yes, they grew up rough. And now one of them is married to my daughter, and she's the happiest she's ever been."

Em and I waited. This was going somewhere, but Mom wasn't going to rush it.

"Now, my other daughter," Mom went on. "I thought she was settled. We all did. Lauren, the girl on the straight path, who knew exactly what she wanted. Okay, she got married a little early. But lots of people do that and it works out just fine. It took me a while to realize that she wasn't very happy at all."

I pulled out the chair behind the front desk and sank into it, my legs weak. "You didn't think I was happy?"

"You said you were," Mom said. "But you worked so much. So much. I know it's funny to hear me say that, considering all the hours I worked while I was married. But the difference was that for a long time your father and I were happy. Really, really happy, raising our daughters together. The reason we both knew we weren't happy anymore was because we knew what it felt like and that feeling was gone." Mom looked at me and smiled. "Anyway, you were doing the best you could. I know the feeling. And when you couldn't have a baby, you just started to fade. You weren't miserable or angry, you just weren't there anymore. There was less and less of you. It's hard to explain."

I blinked tears from my eyes. "Well, thanks for the therapy session. This was great, Mom. Just great."

"I'm not finished yet," Mom said. "When you split from Vic, I knew you were hurting, but there was a little more of you again. And then suddenly, out of the blue, there you were." She reached out and gestured to me, as if I was an amazing item on display. "My Lauren. She just blossomed. She was feisty and funny and oh, so incredibly beautiful. And I realized someone was making my daughter happy. Really happy." She laughed. "And then I heard the rumors and realized I had yet another Riggs brother to thank."

I looked away. I was tired of pretending it wasn't happening. "Do you want to know the truth?" I asked them.

"Of course we want to know the truth, honey," my mother said. "We know you're a private person, but this is a big deal. We want to help."

So I told them. About the baby deal. About how it ended up

being more for both of us. About how it turned out that Dex and I were best friends and lovers and everything in between. About how he'd been taken away from me for a while, and then I found out I wasn't pregnant after all. And the fact that I wasn't going to have a baby hurt—but the fact that I wasn't going to have Dex's baby hurt even more.

When I finished, my sister gave me one of her rare hugs, and I let her do it. My mother watched us, and when Emily let me go she said, "Well, that makes my decision easier."

"What decision?" I asked her.

"To tell you where he is."

I went still, staring at her.

"The verdict came down thirty minutes ago," Mom said. "Guilty on all counts for both men. They're going to prison, which means the state is finished with Dex."

"He's coming home?" I said.

"Not tonight," Mom said. "In the morning. They've put him in a motel tonight and kept his phone from him. I think it's to keep him away from the press, though as of tomorrow if he wants to talk to a reporter there's nothing they can do."

"They don't know Dex very well," I said. "Dex would rather skin himself alive than talk to a reporter."

"True," Mom said. "In the meantime..." She pulled a folded piece of paper from her pocket and handed it to me. "It sometimes pays to know people in law enforcement."

I opened the paper and saw the name of a motel, an address, and a room number. "Oh, my God, Mom," I said.

"They're taking him there any minute. I just wanted to make sure my hunch was right and this was something you wanted." She sighed. "I guess I'm having another Riggs boy over to dinner. I may as well invite all of them at this rate."

I grabbed my mother, hugged her, and kissed her. I turned to Emily, but she was already holding out my coat. "Go," she said.

"Thank you," I said. "Thank you both." And I turned and raced out the door.

TWENTY-THREE

Dex

I HAD NEVER BEEN SO tired in my fucking life. I sat on the chair in my hotel room—it felt like I'd been here since birth—and listened to the cops around me celebrating when the verdict came down. Someone brought a six pack of beer. Even Andre and some of the other security guards high fived. Me, I could feel nothing.

Some bigwig in a suit came to see me. "Dex Riggs," he said, shaking my hand. Who was he? The DA, maybe. I wasn't listening when he introduced himself. He was tall, silver-haired, confident, smooth. "I have to thank you for your help with all of this," he said, as if *all of this* was a party he was putting on. "It was a team effort, no doubt about it. But your testimony was the nail in the coffin. Definitely the nail in the coffin, sir."

"Okay," I said.

MAKE ME BEG   151

"I realize we have some cleanup to do. But I think we're on the right path."

What was he even saying? "Yeah. That's great. Can I go home now?"

Another guy in a suit stepped up to the silver-haired guy and whispered in his ear.

"Soon, very soon," the silver-haired guy said. "We have a bit of a situation with reporters and it's probably best that you don't talk to them. But we'll make sure you get home safe before too much longer."

They made me sign papers—something about how I promised not to sue them, how I promised not to publish a book— as if I would ever in my life publish a fucking book. Seriously. Before long I was put into the back of an unmarked car with two security guards driving it, a grocery bag with my belongings in it in my lap. We drove into the suburbs somewhere and they checked me into a motel.

"What about my phone?" I asked when they unlocked the room and let me in, bag in hand.

"Not yet," one of them said. "We'll courier it to you. You're checked in for tonight."

"Yeah? And then what?"

The security guard shrugged. "You're on your own. So long, Riggs."

As the door closed behind him, I realized this was where the great State of Michigan had left me after three weeks of service. Alone in a motel the middle of nowhere on a dark, freezing night, my only belongings a grocery bag with some underwear, socks, and a toothbrush.

Fuck it. I was finally free.

I dropped the bag and went straight to the phone on the nightstand. I tried calling Lauren's number, but all I got was a series of electronic clicks in my ear. I tried calling Luke's number and got the same thing.

Had they disabled the phone line in my room somehow? "Nice try, assholes," I said. I had no car, no phone, and my wallet had only a little bit of money, but I would start with the front desk. If they wouldn't help, I'd find a phone booth. Hell, I'd walk all the way back to Westlake if I had to. There was no fucking way I was staying here.

I was grabbing my coat again when there was a knock on the door. "What the fuck do you want now?" I said as I opened it.

Lauren stood there.

She was wearing jeans and a winter coat and her hair was in a ponytail. Windblown wisps of honey-blonde hair framed her face. She was beautiful and for a second she wasn't even fucking real. Then she launched herself through the door and into my arms.

I couldn't do anything except hold on. She smelled like winter and woman and Lauren. I buried my face in her neck and inhaled.

After a long minute I collected myself enough to pull back and close the door behind us. "How did you know where I was?" I asked her.

Her face was perfect, her skin luminous in the dim light from the lamp. "I had a tip from a cop," she said.

Her mother. The fact that Nora Parker could find out where they'd left me wasn't a surprise. The fact that she'd given Lauren the information was. I should probably say something else, but I didn't. Instead I cupped Lauren's face in my hands and kissed her.

She tasted so good. I took my time and kissed her exactly how I wanted, taking her in. I'd been fucking starving for this woman, and I didn't care if she knew it.

When we broke off, her breath was short and her eyes were

dark as she opened them and looked at me. "Are you okay?" she asked me.

"Me?" I said. "I'm indestructible, like a cockroach. It's you I'm worried about." I stroked her cheekbone with my thumb. "Lauren, I am so fucking sorry."

She blinked. "Sorry? For what?"

"For not being there when you needed me." That phone call, with Lauren sobbing on the other end, haunted my dreams. I stroked her cheekbone again. "I'm sorry you didn't get what you wanted."

A flinch crossed her expression, and I knew I'd hit a nerve. I always knew when Lauren was hurting. To me it was so fucking obvious.

"I'm okay, Dex," she said, and her eyes told me she wasn't lying to me. "It was hard, but I can handle it. I'll be okay." She smiled a little. "I'm a little like a cockroach, too."

She was strong. She was slim and sweet, but underneath she was made of nothing but steel. But she was so much better than me. "Not even close to the same thing," I said.

"I'm better now that I have you back," she said, her voice ending on that dreamy sigh I liked so much. "I saw you on TV. You were amazing. Everyone says you were brilliant in court."

I shook my head. "I just told the truth, that's all. I should have done it a long time ago."

"You had good reasons."

I had. I couldn't lie—it was good to know that Preakness and Black were gone for a long time, that Rick's wife and kids were safe. Everything was so complicated that I hadn't let myself feel relief. I took a breath and felt something loosen in me, like a muscle that had been knotted for years. "It's over," I said to Lauren.

Her eyebrows went up. "Yeah, it is. Didn't you hear the part about the guilty verdict?"

I stepped back and rubbed a hand over my face. How long had I been living with what Preakness and Black had done, with what I had done? With the memory of that threat? How many hours of sleep had I lost? How many nights had I gotten drunk and high in order to forget? Now I was free of it.

What the hell was I supposed to do now?

I looked at the woman in front of me. She unzipped her coat and shrugged it off. Well, that was one part of the answer.

I could focus on being someone Lauren Parker might like to be with. If I was lucky.

"You're staying?" I asked as she tossed her coat on a chair. "I figured we'd get the hell out of here as fast as we can."

"We may as well stay," she said. "I just drove all the way from Westlake. We'll go home in the morning." She gave me a look from under her lashes. "Besides, the room is already paid for, right?"

I laughed. "Staying in a government-paid motel room isn't as glamorous as it sounds. Trust me, I'm an expert."

"Well, you haven't stayed in one with me," she said with perfect logic. She kicked off her boots and looked around. "That's all your luggage?" she asked, pointing at my grocery bag.

"That's it." I'd left the suit in the closet in the last hotel room —on purpose. Being on the witness stand was not a good memory, and I never wanted to see that suit again. "I told you, this wasn't a luxury trip." I walked to the bed and sat on the edge, my elbows on my knees. "Fill me in, Parker. I haven't had a phone in three weeks. When they give me my phone back, I might throw a fucking parade."

She sat on the edge of the bed next to me and ran through everything. The Porsche client had gotten jumpy when he heard I was going to court in a high-profile corruption case, but Ryan had talked him out of taking his business elsewhere. He'd continued working on the car without me, but it was slow. Luke and Jace had pitched in when they could, but business at both of the Riggs Auto locations was brisk with me on the news. Both places had a lineup of customers.

"Everyone is talking about you in Westlake," Lauren said. "Everyone we went to high school with, every teacher, every guy you ever beat up."

I ran my left thumb over the uneven knuckles of my right hand. I'd gotten in a lot of fights in high school, all of which I'd won. "For the record, most of them had it coming."

"I know," she said with a smile that made me go hot. That was not Lauren's good-girl smile. It wasn't her I'm-always-polite smile. No, that smile was the one that only I got—and even then, only when I'd earned it. "I never thought you were as bad as everyone said you were, you know."

"I was worse."

"No way. If you were that bad, I wouldn't have let you be my first kiss."

I froze. "What?"

"I didn't tell you?" she said innocently, her eyes wide. "Oh, well, you were. I'd never been kissed before that night."

She wasn't bullshitting. I'd been her first kiss, and I'd had no idea. "Jesus, Parker," I said, running a hand through my hair. "Give a guy a heads up. If I'd known that I would've tried harder or something."

"If you'd known that, you wouldn't have done it. Which is why I didn't tell you."

She was right. If she'd told me that night that she'd never been kissed before, I would have kicked her ass out the door without touching her. It would have hurt, but I still would have done it. "Now I'm trying to remember what I did," I said. "It was good, right? I remember using tongue."

"Oh, there was definitely tongue," she said, her voice wistful.

"Oh, hell." I scrubbed my hand over my face. "I'm trying to

remember what I was doing that night. I went into the bedroom to change my shirt, and when I came out, there you were."

"You were changing your *shirt?*" She sounded shocked.

I pulled back and looked at her. "What did you think I was doing?"

"Something nefarious. I was sixteen and I was sneaking into your party, and you were *Dex Riggs.*" She shook her head. "When Dex Riggs comes out of a bedroom in the middle of one of his parties, you imagine an orgy in there or something."

It would have been funny if it wasn't so weird. "You're saying that you thought I was having an orgy, and you kissed me anyway?"

"You kissed me," she reminded me. "I just participated."

"Fine. You thought I'd had an orgy, and you let me kiss you." When she shrugged, I said, "Okay, well, that's a little fucking strange. But for the record there was no orgy."

"You mean, no orgy *that night.*"

I shook my head. "I'm not an orgy guy, Parker. Jesus. I knew I had a bad reputation in Westlake, but I didn't think it was that bad."

"It was bad," Lauren said firmly. "Like orgy bad. But this whole trial has changed things. I think you might almost be rehabilitated."

"Never gonna happen," I said. "It's probably—What are you doing?"

She had gotten up and was straddling my lap. "I'm making a move," she said, putting her hands on my chest and pushing me gently back so I was lying on the bed. "You made the first move ten years ago. It's my turn."

She braced herself over me, and I had to curl my hands into fists so I wouldn't rip her clothes off. I wanted her so fucking bad. "I'm trying to be nice here," I said. "You just went through something shitty, and I've been away for three weeks, and according to the calendar you might still be on your period."

Lauren reached behind her head and pulled the elastic out of her ponytail, letting her hair fall. "I'm finished my period, Dex, but thanks for remembering." She leaned down and kissed me.

I had no defenses. I reached up into her soft hair and cupped her, going long and deep. She sucked my tongue and my body went haywire. It didn't matter that we were on a creaking bed in a cheap hotel room in the middle of nowhere. Everything was good when I had Lauren. Everything was so fucking good.

I ran my hands down over her curves, moved under her sweater and cupped her breasts over her thin T-shirt. She sighed and nibbled my lip as her hand went to my belt and the buttons on my jeans.

And I laid it out there. I had to. After everything we'd been through, I had no choice. "Tell me what this is," I said to her, so close I felt her breath on me. "Be honest with me, Parker. If this is you wanting a baby, I'm willing to try again. But we both know it isn't the right time."

Lauren paused, braced over me, her hand on the buttons of my jeans, her hair falling in soft waves. Her eyes met mine. "I do," she said. "I do want a baby, Dex. Our baby. I want to try again."

I swallowed. I couldn't speak. If she'd said no, I had no idea what I would do.

"But that isn't what this is," she said. "It's been three weeks, and I missed you like crazy. I was miserable. I felt like I was losing my mind."

I knew how she felt. "I missed you so fucking much I felt like I was turned inside out," I said.

She sighed, then leaned down and brushed her lips against mine. "Then let's start new," she said. "Come back to Westlake and be with me. No baby agreement. No bullshit. Just Lauren Parker and Dex Riggs as a couple. For real. You and me."

"You want that?" I asked her, my voice rough. "Because it might be a bumpy ride."

She smiled at me, that Lauren smile that made me crazy. "I can handle it. Can you?"

I was hers. I was so fucking hers. She just didn't know it yet. "Get ready, Parker," I said. "You and me."

Lauren leaned down to kiss me again. "You and me, Dex," she said. "Forever."

THE RIGGS BROTHERS EPILOGUE

Two Years Later

Emily

"I think we should throw a party," I said.

I was watching my husband, Luke Riggs. He was in our back yard, finishing a repair to our back deck. It was hot out, and I was sitting in a chair on the deck with a frosty glass of iced tea. As I sipped I watched Luke, sweaty and shirtless, swing a hammer.

It was literally the best way any woman had ever spent an afternoon.

"We don't need to throw a party, Em," Luke said in his low, masculine growl. That sound still sent shivers up my spine. He picked up another nail and put it in place. "People are here all the time anyway."

It was true. We had a big house, a big yard, and a guest house.

We had brothers and sisters and in-laws who lived minutes away. The fact was, a lot of them spent time here. It was just that kind of place. We had made it that kind of place.

"We do need to throw a party," I said, watching as our dog, Sonny, bounded up to Luke, sniffed his armpit, and bounded away again. To Sonny, anything happening in the backyard was a doggy game. "It's nice to have people over, but we need to do something official. And the family has something to celebrate."

Luke grunted. He drove the nail into the wood with one swing, because my husband was basically walking porn. Good God. Sonny bounded up again, and Luke pushed his nose gently away before he hurt himself. "I suppose, if that's what you want. What do you suggest?"

"A barbecue," I said, not taking my eyes off his muscles as he worked. I liked to ogle my husband, I didn't like to stop, and I didn't care who knew it. "Streamers. Music. Games for the kids. You know, have them hit badminton birdies or throw bean bags or something."

Luke glanced up at me, a smile in his eyes. "There's only one kid big enough to do any of those things."

"So far," I corrected him, though he was technically right. Ryan's son Dylan was almost ten, so he could play all the games. Ryan and Kate had another baby, a daughter named Ella who was only one. And Dex and Lauren.... Well Dex and Lauren had a newborn. A baby boy named Josh. After years of trying, they had finally had a baby at last. It was all my sister ever wanted, and she was finally a mother.

Just thinking about it made my eyes sting with tears.

Luke and I didn't have kids yet. That was by mutual agreement. We had a lot of other things going on: both of us ran our own businesses, and we were fixing up the house. We liked to take road trips together whenever we could swing the time, getting into Luke's Charger and driving wherever the wind took us for weeks at a time. For the past two years I knew I could die happy, sitting in the passenger seat, switching the radio station while Luke was at the wheel. It was my idea of bliss.

Plus, we had Sonny. And we had become the aunt and uncle who were always good to babysit, always ready to take Dylan to the movies or pick him up from camp. We were the aunt and uncle who could be trusted with baby Ella, even overnight, when Ryan and Kate needed a break. Dylan had a bedroom in the house that was kept for him, and Ella would have one too. So would baby Josh in time.

And to be honest, I was a bit of a selfish bitch when it came to my husband. He was hot and he was wonderful, and I liked having him all to myself. I liked having all of his attention. I liked having peace and quiet and lots of sleep and the freedom to jump him whenever I felt like it. Our life was full, and our life was good.

Still... I watched his perfect back as he bent to get another nail. I was almost thirty, and I was starting to feel that clock ticking inside me like a freaking cliché.

"Luke," I said.

"Yeah?" He looked over his shoulder, distracted. "Quit that, you stupid dog." Sonny was chasing his tail, growling at it like it was an enemy. "For fuck's sake, I've never seen anyone so idiotic."

"Sonny isn't stupid," I chided him. "He's just high-spirited. Shaming him is bad for his self-esteem."

"Yeah?" Luke said, watching as Sonny snapped at his tail and then tore around the yard, trying to get away from whatever was biting him. "You sure about that?"

Okay, fine. Sonny was a mutt we'd gotten from a high-kill shelter, and he had no pedigree to speak of. He was a muddy black color with a few white spots, and he loved a chew toy in the shape of a banana above all other things. But he was loving, he had no concept of anger or mistrust, and he was great with the kids, no matter how much Ella liked to grab his fur with her little fists.

"I was going to say something important," I reminded Luke.

He turned back to the deck. "Yeah, I know. About a party."

"No, not about that. About something else."

"Something else? Jesus Em, I can't keep up. What is it now?"

"Do you think we should have a baby?"

He stopped what he was doing and looked at me.

I suddenly felt nervous. The last time we had talked about this was maybe a year ago, and it hadn't come up since. Maybe he thought it was never going to come up again. I sipped my iced tea, my heart in my throat all of a sudden.

"Is that what you want?" Luke asked me.

It was a careful question, one that gave nothing away.

"Well, you know," I said, clearing my throat. I couldn't back out now, pretend I hadn't said it. "Um, I was just thinking, I'm almost thirty—"

"You're twenty-eight."

"That's almost thirty. Totally." I cleared my throat again. "Anyway, if we started now, or soon, and if I got pregnant, I'd be thirty by the time the baby is born. And then, you know, if we want to have another one—"

"*Another* one?"

"Yes, well, we'd probably wait a few years for baby number two, which by the time it's born puts me closer to thirty-five. Which is almost old."

He blinked once. "Em, thirty-five is not old."

"It is in baby-making years. At least for women. This is how we women have to think about it, Luke. You men get to be Hugh Hefner and knock women up until you're ninety. Women can't think that way. We have baby-making years, and we have to make the most of them."

Luke sat back on his haunches, putting his tools down and running a hand through his hair. "Baby-making years. Okay."

"It's true. And that's if I get pregnant easily. But Lauren didn't." I swallowed, thinking of the years my twin had spent trying to get pregnant. Josh had finally happened after their second round of IVF. "What if I have the same problems she did? It could be a few years before it happens, if it happens at all. And if I wait too late in my baby-making years, the odds get worse."

Luke leaned over and grabbed his T-shirt where he'd dropped it on the ground. He stood up, putting the shirt on, and came toward me on the deck. He reached out his hand and I took it, standing up.

"You're worried about this?" he asked me, his face serious. "This has been on your mind?"

"A little, yes." I licked my lip. "Sometimes. Not all the time. Mostly recently. It's a thing that's crossed my mind." I was babbling, but Luke didn't care. He never cared when I did stupid things, which was why I loved him so much.

"You're worried about it," he said, translating my babbling.

"It's fine. You know, if you don't want to. It isn't just about me. A baby is a big thing."

"Em."

"It'll stretch our finances a bit," I went on. "I know that. But I think we can handle it. I could take some time off from the salon. My parents will be able to help out. We might not need full time day care."

"Em. Look at me."

I looked up at him. I'd known Luke Riggs since I was seventeen. He was the first man I'd ever slept with, the man I'd never get enough of. He might be a bad boy from the wrong side of the tracks, but to me he was amazing. I wanted to be the mother of his kids. At least, I wanted to try.

"Yes," I said, looking at his face and knowing the truth. "I want to."

He searched my face, and then the corners of his eyes crinkled. "Okay then. We'll do it."

I couldn't think of anything to say. I reached up, put my arms around his neck, and kissed him. When I pulled back I said, "I'm throwing my pills away right now."

"Just one baby to start, okay?" Luke said. "Seriously."

I leaned up and kissed him again, then pulled away and said, "I love you, Luke Riggs."

"I love you, too."

"Oh, and I'm still throwing a party."

This time he leaned down and kissed me. "Throw your party," he said when he finished. "Let's have everyone over to celebrate."

Tara

"That's him?" said my new assistant, Anita, as she looked out the window. "For real?"

I looked past her shoulder. We were in my second-floor office, looking down over the street. Below us a car had parked in one of the streetside spots and a man got out. He was big, dark-haired, wearing jeans and black T-shirt in summer, like a biker. Even from here I could see the silver rings on his fingers.

"That's him," I said. "That's my husband."

Anita stared at him, speechless as he paid the meter and locked the car.

"It's best if I point him out to you," I said. "Whenever

someone new starts in the office and Jace comes in, they're tempted to call security. Not everyone believes him when he says we're married."

"Oh my Lord," Anita said as Jace circled the hood of the car and walked toward the office doors. He was completely unaware he was being ogled, and I knew it wasn't an act. I'd been married to Jace for nearly two years now, I'd seen him get ogled dozens of times, and not once had he caught on. He was completely oblivious. Which, really, was fine with me.

"He used to be my client," I told Anita. "That's how I met him. When I counseled him after he got out of prison."

"Oh my Lord," she said again. "You poached from the client pool. And you seemed so nice."

I laughed, stepping away from the window. "I am nice."

"Uh huh," she said, stepping away herself now that Jace was no longer in view. She looked around the office, at my desk, at the chair and the sofa. "Please tell me you've never done it in here with that beast of a man. Or I'll have to get the wipes from my purse."

I held up my hand like a Girl Scout. "I swear we've never had sex in this office." We'd done it in the bathroom down the hall—after hours, of course—but she didn't ask about that, so I wasn't lying.

"Uh huh," Anita said again. "I've seen that innocent look on my boys' faces, too, and I never believe it there either. Is he nice, at least?"

I lowered my hand. "He's nice," I said. "Really nice. You wouldn't believe how nice he is, honestly."

"He looks like a guy from *Sons of Anarchy*," Anita said.

"Would you believe me if I told you he does most of the grocery shopping and the housework? Because it's true."

She shook her head, still not convinced. "I have a hard time picturing someone like that scrubbing toilets."

"Who scrubs toilets?" Jace appeared in the open doorway of the office and leaned a shoulder on the doorframe. He looked at me, his eyes going warm, and then he looked at Anita. "Hi, I'm Jace."

"Anita." She took his hand and shook it, his big hand gently dwarfing hers. She let him go and pointed at me. "According to her, the toilet scrubber is you."

Jace looked pained and scratched his forehead. "You're not supposed to tell people that," he said to me. "It ruins my manly persona."

And that was when it happened. It was the same thing that always happened when a woman met Jace, whether she was nine or ninety. Sometimes it happened right away, and sometimes it happened a little later, but it was always the same. Anita got a soft, mushy look on her face, and I knew she was smitten with my husband.

"Well, you're just sweet," she said. "Goodness."

"I'm not sweet," he argued. "I'm intimidating."

Anita laughed, and I sighed. The Jace effect. It was ridiculous. He didn't even have to try.

She turned to me. "Anyone who calls security on this one is a straight-up fool," she declared, "and I'll kick their butt myself. Now I'm going home. I'll see you all later." She looked around the office and narrowed her eyes at me. "I'm still keeping wipes in my purse, though."

"What was that about?" Jace asked when she'd left. He came all the way into the office, closing the door behind him. "The wipes thing?"

I gathered my own purse and powered my computer down, feeling the same shiver of excitement I always felt around Jace. I'd felt it the very first time he walked in for a counseling session, and marriage hadn't changed the feeling one bit.

He was big, my husband. Muscled. His hair was a bit long on

top, and he had a dark, trim beard on his jaw. Gorgeous hands with rings on them. Nice arms. But as always it was his eyes that got me. Dark-lashed, expressive, intelligent. Beautiful eyes, really, though he hated to hear it. So I kept my observations to myself.

"She thinks we have sex in the office," I explained to him. "I told her we don't, but she doesn't believe me."

Jace came up behind me and put a gentle hand around my waist. "Only because you say no," he teased me.

"Because I have to work in here." I straightened and turned to face him, feeling his firm arm around my waist. "I can't work at this desk if..." I gestured to it. "You know."

"I know," he said, smiling. "I get it."

He did get it. That was the thing. I had moved up at the counseling centre to be a supervising counselor, and in a few months I'd be in line for yet another promotion. I made good money, and I took my career seriously. And as much as I loved my husband, I couldn't make light of my career by banging him in my office. So he didn't ask me to.

"Besides," Jace said, "there are plenty of other places to do it. Did you tell her about the bathroom?"

"Of course not," I said, letting him pull me close so our bodies were flush. "She likes you."

"She seems nice," he said. He leaned down and kissed me gently, his lips making my skin tingle. "You like me," he said.

"A little," I admitted. Put my arms around his neck and leaned up close to him. I was tall, but Jace was taller. "You like me, too."

"A little."

We kissed longer this time. It was the best thing, realizing that my work—work I loved—was done for the day, and I had a whole evening with this man. Just him and me. I kept waiting for the excitement, the first-date anticipation, to end, and it never did.

I pulled away. "I remembered something I have to tell you," I said.

"What is it?"

"Two things, actually. First, we're going to a barbecue at Luke and Emily's tomorrow."

"Okay. What's the other thing?"

"I have to go to Chicago in two weeks."

"Another conference?"

I nodded. "Sorry, it's important."

My job meant that I needed to be constantly learning, because there was always new research that evolved the best counseling techniques. It also meant I needed to be in touch with other counseling centers—the more the better, because we shared information. I'd already been to two conferences this year. They were valuable and sometimes fun, but I hated being away from Jace so much.

Jace, I'd learned, was a bit of a homebody. He had mixed feelings about Westlake, but it was his home. He was also an ex-con, and ex-cons sometimes got hassled when they flew, even domestically. So flying was not Jace's favorite thing. When he got the itch to travel, which was rarely, he preferred to drive.

But he'd never given me a hard time about my traveling. We'd decided early on that neither of us was interested in having kids— I liked my career too much, and Jace said that since all of his brothers would probably have kids sooner or later, being an uncle was plenty for him. So sometimes I left town for work, and Jace took care of everything at home. He took care of things, too, when I worked long hours. And let me tell you, there was nothing better than coming home from a trip or a long day to find a hot biker-looking guy waiting for you with a stocked fridge. I was well aware I had the best deal in womankind.

Jace looked thoughtful. "How long will you be gone?" he asked me.

"Five days." I let my palms stroke his chest. I hated even thinking about it.

"Has the lovely Anita booked your flight yet?"

I looked up at him. "What are you thinking?"

Jace shrugged, then scratched his jaw. "Maybe I'll come. I've always wanted to see Chicago."

"Really?" My heart jumped. "That would be wonderful."

"You can do what you need to do at the conference. I won't be in your way." He smiled at me. "We never did have a honeymoon."

He was right. We'd gotten married and gone straight back to work, him at Riggs Auto—where he did the managing, the marketing, and the books—and me at the counseling center. "This can be our honeymoon, then."

"Chicago in summer while you're working isn't exactly a honeymoon."

"We'll make it one." I leaned up and kissed him. "I don't care where I am, as long as I'm with you, Jace Riggs."

He gave me an amused grin. "You've been watching Hallmark movies again."

I put my arms around his neck and kissed him again. "You love it when I watch Hallmark movies. Let's go home."

Kate

"Ryan Riggs," I growled, trying not to scream. "*Get out here and get your daughter.*"

It was hot. Boiling hot, the sun baking down mercilessly from a cloudless sky. I was standing in our driveway with sweat beading on my neck and between my boobs. Even my hair was sweating. I was loading everything into the car for Luke and Emily's party—food, drinks, extra food and drinks, two big bags of baby supplies. I was also trying to wrestle a cranky, livid one-year-old girl into her car seat while she flailed and screamed at the top of her lungs. And so far, I was doing all of it alone.

I was going to kill him.

"Just sit still," I begged Ella, my daughter, as I tried to get the complicated straps untangled across her little body. She paid no attention. Instead she arched her back straight out of the seat, pushing the straps off and yelling so loud her face went red.

I glanced up and down the street, wondering if one of the neighbors was about to call Child Protective Services on the woman who was seemingly murdering a baby in broad daylight.

Nothing worked. Not the sippy cup, not the favorite toy. Not a stern, commanding voice or a pleading one. I was tired of dealing with this problem while Ryan did—what the hell *was* he doing, anyway?

"Ryan Riggs!" I shouted again. "Get out here!"

Finally the front door of the house opened. First out was Dylan, our nine-year-old (almost ten, because that was important) son, wearing a baseball cap and a slightly scared expression when he saw my face. "You're in trouble, Dad," he said. "Shotgun." He bolted to the car and took the front passenger seat.

Next out the door, sauntering like he was on a freaking vacation, was Ryan Riggs—former baseball player, current restorer of classic cars, Dylan and Ella's father, and my husband. He was cool and gorgeous and spectacular. Even in jeans and a gray tee, he looked like he had stepped from the cover of a men's magazine. I could have gleefully stuck a knife in his chest.

"What's the emergency?" he said, as if there wasn't a little girl screaming blue murder, drowning us all out.

I stepped back from the car seat with the screeching girl in it. "That," I said, pointing to Ella, "is your problem. I'm done."

His eyebrows went up, as if he'd just noticed he had a daughter. "Okay," he said, locking the door behind him and coming down the steps. He was even carrying a bottle of iced tea, so cold there was condensation dripping off it. I could have killed him for that, too.

Ryan came closer and looked me up and down. I had tied my hair up off my neck and I was wearing a maxi sundress with spaghetti straps. Maxi dresses were my go-to this summer, because I'd gained weight while pregnant with Ella and no matter how hard I tried, the weight was still sticking like glue. My boobs were still bigger than they used to be, and so were my ass and my hips. Ryan claimed he liked it, but right now he was looking at a hot, sweaty, overtired, exhausted mother who felt like the fattest whale on the planet.

He finally clued in. "Here," he said, handing me the cold bottle of iced tea. As I opened and swigged it, he leaned into the car. "Hey, baby," he said in a soft voice. He undid Ella's straps and lifted her out of the seat.

She immediately stopped screaming. The silence was so profound my ears practically rang. Ryan straightened, holding her, and she dug her face into his shoulder, whimpering softly.

"Well, well," he said to her, wiping her tears from her cheeks with his thumb. "What's the fuss? Time to be quiet, honey."

Ella sighed and closed her eyes.

I drank more iced tea, feeling tears stinging my eyes. I fought them back. I was weirdly emotional these days.

"Are you okay?" Ryan asked me.

I emptied the bottle. "Do you really want me to answer that question?"

"Maybe not," he admitted. He looked down at Ella, whose

face was slowly losing its bright-red hue. "I think she was just hot and tired."

"I know the feeling." I sighed, looking at them. Jesus, it was hard to stay mad. Ryan had her in the crook of his arm, which made his bicep flex in the best possible way. Ella was wearing a purple ballet outfit, complete with tutu—it was a party, so I let her wear whatever she wanted—and was snuggled in to her father's shoulder in perfect bliss now, as if that was what she wanted all along. The two of them together gave me a familiar sensation in my belly that I recognized as my ovaries exploding.

I caught Ryan's gaze moving down and up me again. "That dress looks good," he said. "Really good."

"Stop," I said.

"It makes your boobs look nice."

"Stop."

"You didn't say stop last night."

I glanced back at the car, where Dylan was sitting in the front seat, scrolling on his tablet. "Your kids are listening."

He smiled at me. "You mean our kids."

I softened a little more. Dylan wasn't biologically mine, but I'd legally adopted him when Ryan and I got married. I was three months pregnant with Ella at the time. "Okay, our kids. Remind me again which one of us wanted a baby?"

"You did," he said. "I remember it perfectly. You made a steak dinner, then told me you wanted a baby. I said okay. Then we went and made one."

I sighed. It was true. I'd gotten pregnant almost right away and the pregnancy had been no problem. Even the birth was quick and uncomplicated. It was everything after that was so hard.

But then I looked at our little girl nestled in the crook of her father's arm, and... my heart just twisted.

THE RIGGS BROTHERS EPILOGUE 173

And Ryan wasn't quite so bad, really. He was actually kind of wonderful. He had experience from raising Dylan, so he took everything to do with kids—sleeplessness, piles of laundry, tantrums, endless mess that was sometimes disgusting—in stride. He was a genius at getting both kids to do what he wanted. And he had no problem with the baby weight. It certainly hadn't affected our sex life.

Still.

"Why is everything so easy for you?" I asked him.

Ryan laughed. He turned to the front passenger window. "Dyl, how easy is it to be my kid?"

"I ate fruit roll-ups for three months when I was six," Dylan said, barely looking up from his tablet. "I'm bored and hungry. Can we go now?"

So we went. First Ryan had to put Ella in the car seat, which she sleepily accepted. Then there was a serious conference about the front seat, because Dylan had called shotgun—shotgun rules were sacred—but I was the mother and I had packed the car myself. The end result was Dylan retreating to the back seat with his sister.

And then we went. Our little family, perfectly imperfect.

It was time for a party.

Lauren

It was a great party. We went crazy with the food and drink, and the barbecue was going nonstop. Jace found some great music to play. Dylan was playing a chase-and-wrestle game with Sonny the dog, which they both loved. Ella was happily grabbing streamers. All in all, it was wonderful.

Still, I was happy to sit in the quiet of one of the upstairs bedrooms, alone.

Not quite alone. I had my three-month-old baby, Josh, in my arms. He'd needed a feeding, and frankly, I'd needed a break.

So we sat there, him and me, as he fed. I looked into his face and stroked his little forehead. When it was just him and me, I could be as sappy as I wanted.

The door opened and Dex came in. He knew Josh's feeding schedule as well as I did. "Everything okay?" he asked quietly.

Josh was finished, so I detached him and covered myself. "Everything's good," I said.

Dex took the baby from me and pulled a towel from the baby bag. He tossed the towel over his shoulder, put Josh in position, and patted his back, waiting for the expected burp. "What?" he said, looking down at me.

I smiled up at him. Dark hair, dark blue eyes, badass attitude —that was Dex. The difference was that he was expertly burping a baby. "You look sweet," I said, because I knew that would drive him crazy.

"I do not look sweet," he said. "I am very fucking cool."

"Don't swear in front of your son."

"He doesn't know words yet."

"I know, but I want to hear Dex Riggs say *fudging*. Just once."

"Dream on, Parker." He paced the room, still trying to coax a burp out of Josh. Josh wriggled uncomfortably, trying to get things moving. "What do you think this party is for? The Fourth of July was a week ago."

"Em says it's because we haven't had a party for Josh yet, but I don't believe her."

Dex's eyebrows went up. "No?"

"No. I think they're going to start trying for a baby."

"Emily told you that?"

"She didn't have to." I waved a hand. "I'm her twin. I can read her freaking mind. Also, I could barely get her to let go of Josh. My sister has baby fever. For sure."

Dex seemed to think that over. "Maybe Luke will have to jizz into a cup," he said. "That would be pretty fucking satisfying, since he ribbed me mercilessly about it."

I sighed. Dex had gone through all the indignities of two IVF treatments without complaint, but his brothers hadn't been able to resist teasing him. "None of you will ever grow up, will you?"

"Nope," he said with a grin.

Josh interrupted his father by finally giving a giant burp, and we both laughed.

We cleaned up the mess and put Josh in his carrier as his eyes drooped closed for a post-feeding nap. I felt my own eyes droop closed, too. People weren't kidding when they said that newborn babies robbed you of sleep. I sat on the bed and curled my feet up onto the coverlet. "Do we have to go back to the party?" I asked.

"You don't," Dex said. I felt him get onto the narrow bed behind my back. "Have a nap. Everyone will understand."

"Just for a minute." I yawned. I felt Dex stroke my hair, then put his arm around my waist.

Every part of me relaxed when he did that. I loved, loved, loved it when he touched me. Even if he just brushed my arm or held my hand. It was sexy but it was everything else, too. After having a baby at long last, we'd had to find our way back to each other, slowly but surely. "I promise we'll have a normal sex life again someday," I said to him.

"Relax, Lauren," he said, kissing the side of my neck. "I'm not going anywhere. Everything's fine."

He was right. Everything was fine with the world. I could

hear my family out the window, laughing and enjoying themselves. And in this quiet room, I had a view of my sleeping son and I had Dex in the bed with me, holding me tight. Protecting me. And I knew he always would.

Yes, I thought as I closed my eyes. *Things are pretty damn wonderful.*

ALSO BY JULIE KRISS

Made in the USA
Middletown, DE
28 December 2018